The Ice Maiden

by

Steve Lockley & Paul Lewis

Limited edition number R̄ārēw *of 250*

The Ice Maiden

by

Steve Lockley & Paul Lewis

Introduction by Tim Lebbon

First published in 2004 by
Pendragon Press
Po Box 12, Maesteg, Mid Glamorgan
South Wales, CF34 0XG, UK

ISBN 0 9538598 1 9

Typesetting by Christopher Teague

Printed & bound in the UK by
Antony Rowe, Eastbourne

Dreaming in Fire and Ice

An introduction by Tim Lebbon

*T*his is a novella about dreams. Good dreams and bad dreams, dreams that hang around for life and those that fade away as quickly as a sigh in the night. It's also about the faith we invest in dreams … and how sometimes those imaginings may be more real than we would really wish to believe.

Tessa has fled London after discovering that her husband was cheating on her. They are divorced, he is out of her life, but the memory of the dreams she had during that most difficult time remains. Was her subconscious really trying to reveal the truth to her, the painful reality that the circumstances were all pointing toward? Or perhaps it was much more than that. Perhaps she did not have to rely on the scraps of evidence – the smell of perfume on her husband's skin, the mysterious phone calls, the 'late nights at the office'.

Maybe she simply *knew* the truth.

So here she is in Bethesda in the Brecon Beacons, teaching art at a local school, trying to fit in, desperate to make a new life for herself. It's a pleasant village, and the school is nice, though many of the teachers are a little cool toward her. Of those who do seem to offer her a welcome one is a creepy letch, and the other … well, he's someone she could get to like.

Desperate to convince herself that she isn't merely running away, Tessa's determination to fit in keeps her set apart. And then the dreams begin again. Burning first, then drowning, choking, the sense that someone is holding her beneath water … and, soon, the certainty that as the dreams continue she will come to see who that someone is.

When a teenaged girl from one of her classes disappears Tessa immediately links the disappearance with her dreams. She comes to believe, very quickly, that when she sleeps she is imagining the girl's murder. And it is guilt more than anything else that leads her to begin investigating.

The dreams grow in frequency and detail – that elusive face, the face of the girl's killer, begins to manifest – and Tessa's hesitant involvement with the missing girl's mother turns it into a very personal quest.

But dreams are fickle things, and our willingness to believe in them is perhaps too strong. Some set the imagination aflame and last forever, while others are ice-cool, forgotten by lunchtime. In this novella of faith and consequence – Tessa's faith in a mysterious power she may have, and the consequence of that faith remaining blind – she attempts to translate and explore her own subconscious messages.

There are surprises in store for Tessa and the reader. Not everything in life is as it seems, so why should dreams be any different? Yet there are clues here as well. And that is what makes this such a great mystery story.

Lockley and Lewis have created a beautifully realised sense of place, the village of Bethesda lovingly wrought, the school and surrounding countryside given a thriving life by these two talented writers. For those of you already aware of their work, you will know that they are now so adept at collaborating that they have created their own collaborative voice. No clumsy changes of style here. The plot moves along smoothly, and the writing is just as seamless.

For those of you who are new to the world of Lockley and Lewis, this is a fine place to begin. Like their novel *The Ragchild* and novella *King of All the Dead*, *The Ice Maiden* is a joy to read, and doubtless only a dreamlike hint of what is yet to come.

Tim Lebbon
Goytre
October 2003

The Ice Maiden

Freezing cold held her in an embrace so powerful that she could not breathe. The sudden, shocking sensation of it made her want to cry out, but she began to choke when she tried. The cold poured into her mouth, invaded her lungs. She fought to free herself but there was no escape. Then darkness filled her vision and she was falling, falling into night ...

"No!"

The shout escaped Tessa's lips as she thrashed around in tangled, sweat-soaked sheets before sitting bolt upright in bed, gasping for breath. Panic still gripped her even with her eyes open wide and familiar surroundings swimming into focus, illuminated by dawn's first tentative intrusions through the curtains.

Just a dream, she told herself. *Just a dream. Just a dream.*

She kept saying it, over and over, the mantra-like repetition helping to calm her jangling nerves. Slowly her breathing steadied and her thumping heart subsided to something approaching its normal rate. Tessa lay back on the bed but did not close her eyes.

It was hardly the first time she'd had a bad dream, but this particular nightmare disturbed her. She could remember no details, only vivid sensations of cold and of choking, as if she were drowning in icy water. It had left her feeling utterly helpless. Even though the central heating timer had kicked in and the bedroom was pleasantly warm, just thinking about that devastating cold made her shiver.

She pushed back the clammy sheets and glanced at the glowing red digits of her bedside alarm clock. Just after six-thirty. It was too early to get up, but in another hour she'd have to start getting ready for work so there was no point trying to sleep. Not that she was certain she wanted to, not if it meant a repeat of that dream.

"Come on Tessa," she said, surprised slightly by the sound of her voice. "Get a grip. Nothing's going to hurt you. Not here."

Sure, but how many times had she told herself that before?

She had felt secure in London, with Jonathan, secure and happy. It had seemed inconceivable that her life would ever change. Until the night she discovered her time with him had been nothing more than a sick joke at her expense.

The irony was that she had always dismissed women who claimed that divorce had shattered their lives. Now she understood. It was not about being dependant on men, and it certainly wasn't about sex. It was about betrayal.

She should have guessed the truth about Jonathan long before he confirmed it. The frequent absences, which he blamed on work. The phone calls which, when answered by Tessa, met only with silence followed by the dialling tone as the caller hung up. And the way he was uncomfortable looking her in the eyes when he talked about why he had to stay on in the office at night, or work at weekends. She couldn't say that the signs had not been there, only that she had chosen not to recognise them.

There had also been the dreams, which she had dismissed as coincidence or a warning from her inner self. If those dreams had meant something, then what was this latest nightmare trying to tell her? That she was suffocating here, in this middle-of-nowhere place? That she had made the wrong decision when she had fled London, looking for the chance to put her life back on track without Jonathan? So far she had not been successful. Okay, so she had a good job, a nice home and a decent income, thanks to her salary and the settlement her solicitor had hammered out for her.

Unfortunately, money did not make her world go round. She had no friends, only acquaintances. She was alone in a cottage large enough to house a family. Instead of having a life, Tessa felt that she simply existed.

"Not now." She forced herself out of bed, limbs stiff and aching. Self-pity at this early hour was not a good way to start the day. Especially a Monday, when going into school after the weekend break was always a daunting prospect.

She pulled back the curtains and stared out at the deserted village. Snow had fallen overnight, dusting the streets and rooftops and capping the peaks of the Beacons in the distance. Tessa loved it here. From the back windows she could see the trees which lay beyond the garden. A path led through them to the lake where she spent hours walking, thinking, mostly trying to figure out when it had started to go wrong with Jonathan, and why. It was so peaceful, with only the sound of her footsteps to break the silence. Her mind was free to wander without interruption. In a way this was what had drawn her to Bethesda; the chance to start afresh, to live in a place where one man's ceiling wasn't another man's floor. Finding a teaching job in a small secondary school in Mid Wales had proved easier than expected. Alone she may be, yet she felt like she was finally home.

Bethesda. Even the name evoked some kind of tranquillity, nestling in the shadows of the Brecon Beacons, yet at the same time sounding vaguely biblical. It was light years away from London and that was exactly how she wanted it. All she needed now was the hurt to go away, for Jonathan to be consigned to a forgotten box in the attic of her memory, and then hopefully she would be able to start living properly again. Tessa was not banking on miracles, for a circle of friends to spring up overnight, or for some handsome stranger to sweep her off her feet. Right then, she didn't care if she never shared her life with another man.

Anything could happen, in time. And she had time to spare.

She pulled on her dressing gown and went downstairs to the kitchen. Ten minutes later she was sitting on the sofa, mug of tea in one hand; it was too early for breakfast.

While she drank she half-watched the GMTV news, not really listening to what the presenter was saying but glad of the company all the same.

" ... *in Tel Aviv a suicide bomber on board a bus has killed nine people and seriously injured almost a dozen others ...*"

The warmth of the fire and the heat of the tea lulled her by stealth. Tessa closed her eyes briefly, mentally ordering herself not to fall asleep. Not that she thought she would, when there was even the slightest chance that she would dream that elusive yet strangely disturbing dream again.

" ... *police say the murder of a young Bristol mother could be linked to others across the country. If so it would be Britain's first serial killings since the days of the Yorkshire Ripper ...*"

It really was time to start moving. Otherwise she'd be late. Not exactly the way to impress the boss so soon into a new job.

"... *an outbreak of the potentially deadly MRSA virus has closed a London hospital for the second time this year ...*"

The sound drifted away. What seemed like a split-second later Tessa felt a scalding hot pain and jerked fully awake. She must have started to drift off. The mug had fallen to the floor, spilling hot tea over her hand on its way. *Shit.*

She hurried into the kitchen and ran cold water over her hand, which stung like hell, cursing all the while. Then she grabbed a towel and went back to the living room to scrub at the tea-stain on the rug. The TV droned on and, irritated by it, Tessa reached out and jabbed the off button. It was nothing but bad news anyway.

At least with the Welsh news you had stories like sightings of the Beast of Brynmawr. Tell anyone in London you'd seen a big cat and they would smile indulgently and probably think you were mad. Here you'd be taken seriously. They believe in things like that around here, she thought. And that made her feel even more that, in Bethesda, she had found her home.

The cottage was on the very outskirts of the village. It was several hundred yards away from the nearest houses, situated at the end of a narrow lane. During her first few weeks there Tessa had felt nervous being alone.

Eventually, though, the place had grown on her. Now she loved the fact that, at the end of each working day, she could shut herself off from the rest of the world. The cottage was so close to the forested hills that Tessa's mobile phone couldn't pick up a signal until she was halfway to the village.

Showered and dressed, her hand barely even sore now, Tessa reversed her Ford Escort out of the drive and set off along the lane. The tyres crunched as she emerged on to Church Road and she kept her speed down, wary of skidding. Above her the sky was a slate-coloured canopy. At this time of the year snow was never too far away. It had rained on Christmas Day; by Boxing Day the snow lay four inches thick.

The road to Builth Wells had been gritted and the going was good. Sod's law. Tessa had left twenty minutes earlier than normal to allow for poor conditions, which meant she would be at St David's School with time to kill.

The school was a product of the seventies; a scattering of two-storey, steel-clad blocks. To the left as she approached the school entrance was the sports hall, a relatively modern addition and designed with a little more flair than the squat, functional blocks of classrooms. Beyond it lay the green expanse of the playing fields, flecked with white.

A stream of children had already started to trickle through the gates by the time Tessa drove into the staff car park. Before long it would turn into a raging torrent when the buses turned up to empty their cargoes of boisterous youngsters.

Tessa got out of the Escort, retrieved her bag from the back seat, then slammed and locked the door.

"Morning, darling," she heard from behind, and closed her eyes, suppressing a groan.

"Morning, Greg," she answered, not particularly wanting to turn round and talk to him directly, but knowing she could not bring herself to be so rude as to just walk away.

Gregory Roberts – Greg, as he insisted on being called – must have so hated the fact that he was in his early forties that he tried to dress like someone ten years younger. Tried, and failed. He was a big man, six foot at least, but overweight. He wore light canvas trousers, which clashed with his trendy walking boots, and a heavy-duty North Face jacket at odds with trousers and boots alike. His blonde hair was slicked savagely back, as if he were punishing it for having the nerve to recede. A gold stud pierced his left ear and he wore rimless glasses which only served to give him a perpetually bug-eyed look. Whenever Tessa noticed his gaze turn her way she always imagined he was mentally undressing her. She had shaken hands with him on her first day at the school and could barely repress a shudder of revulsion when she recalled that it had felt like squeezing a bunch of raw sausages. His smile was more of a sneer, which reinforced Tessa's perception of him as the kind of man who dedicated every moment of his free time to jerking off at internet porn.

She was used of being called all kinds of names; love, chuck, duck, any number of regional expressions of friendly affection. None of them bothered her in the slightest. But Greg's *darling* sent a shiver down her spine. Maybe because that was what Jonathan used to call her. It had been nice then, before it had all turned sour.

"How'd your weekend go?"

"Fine," Tessa called over her shoulder, walking away towards the main doors and hoping Greg would take the hint.

He didn't. Instead he fell in beside her, matching her pace. An oversized sports bag hung heavily over his shoulder.

"Get up to anything exciting?" he asked.

"Nothing exciting ever happens in Bethesda."

"Well, if you're ever at a loss, you've got my number." He had insisted on writing it down for her that first time they'd met; Tessa had thrown it away the same day. "Maybe I could call round. We could ... I don't know. Do something."

His lip had curled into that awful sneer. Maybe he was, in his own way, just trying to be friendly. Somehow Tessa doubted it.

"Thanks. I'll bear that in mind. But, you know, what with marking and housework I just don't seem to have much time free these days."

The words sounded as hollow as her stomach felt at the thought of what a date with him might involve. It would have been better to tell him straight that she wasn't interested.

A small group of teenage girls passed by, chatting and laughing loudly. Tessa saw Greg's eyes flick towards them and his tongue briefly darted out to moisten his lips. Just as well it was so cold, she thought, otherwise they would have been wearing skirts rather than trousers. At least now their dignity was intact, whether they knew it or not.

"I'm going to take this lot straight up to the lab."

For a second Tessa thought he meant the girls. Then she noticed him switching the bag from one shoulder to the other.

"Okay."

"See you later."

Tessa hoped he wouldn't.

"Oh, and I mean what I said. Any time you're at a loose end, just give me a bell. Even if it's just for a game of badminton."

Tessa wished she had never mentioned she played. "Sure."

Greg veered off towards one of the side entrances, the closest route to the physics lab, his personal domain. Tessa felt herself relax the moment he was out of sight. He was a letch, a middle aged letch who apparently did not care whether he was lusting after schoolgirls or grown women. Suddenly feeling the cold through her fleece, she hurried to the main doors and into the blissfully warm corridor.

Pupils smiled at her as she walked towards the staff room; a couple gave a breezy 'Hi Miss' as they passed. Not for the first time, Tessa sensed she had made the right choice in opting to live and work as far from London as possible. Her old school had been fine but she'd heard horror stories about some of the others, especially those in the inner city. Teachers threatened with knives, sometimes even assaulted. St David's was an ocean of calm in comparison. Sure, there was the odd bad apple but the majority of the kids were well adjusted and well behaved. They seemed to like her and they worked hard. For an art teacher that was pretty much all you could hope for.

She remembered her own school days. Art had been one of the few subjects which had come naturally to her. Others had struggled, and they often had their work ridiculed in front of the class. When Tessa had decided she wanted to be a teacher she had vowed she would never treat any of her pupils like that. All they had to do was try their best.

Reaching the staff room, she pushed open the door and was immediately assailed by a babble of excited voices. Heads swung towards her at the sound of the squealing hinges and for one moment Tessa was certain they had been talking about her. Then the conversation – which, she quickly realised, was a series of conversations, cutting across each other – picked up again and she felt a wave of relief. *Getting paranoid.*

The staff room was painted a pastel yellow and was filled with mismatched furniture; old sofas which sagged in the middle, armchairs and hard wooden chairs, with small tables dotted here and there. It looked like someone had raided a second-hand shop.

It was still quite early so a few of the armchairs were free. Tessa dumped her bag on one of them and headed for the coffee machine. A few of the others brought their own supplies, jealously guarding jars of Nescafe and whitener as if they were precious treasure. Tessa thought that was too much trouble. The machine coffee was surprisingly good and only cost twenty pence a go.

As she retrieved the full cup from the dispenser she noticed Mike Jenkins making his way towards her. His face, usually smiling and friendly, now appeared troubled. "Have you heard?"

"Heard what?"

"About Claire Marshall."

Tessa's stomach tightened. Claire was a bright kid, a naturally talented artist but touchingly modest with it. She was as happy helping others not as gifted with their work as she was getting on with her own. From the tone of Mike's voice and the look on his face it was blatantly obvious that the news was not good.

"What about her?"

"She's gone missing. Went out yesterday morning, told her mother she was going round to a friend's house. Never came home. Her mother rang in. Distraught, as you can imagine."

"Jesus," Tessa said softly.

"The police have been to see her. They want to talk to Claire's friends. Some of us too, I wouldn't mind betting."

Tessa put the coffee cup down on the nearest table; her hands were trembling. "Do they think they'll find her?"

It was a stupid question, but she had to say something to distract herself from the onslaught of emotions she was experiencing. Claire Marshall was a pretty girl. Tall and blonde, she could turn any man's head. Of course, there could be a mundane explanation, but whenever she heard stories like this on the news Tessa always feared the worst.

If Mike thought the question stupid he didn't show it. "I reckon they'll be optimistic on the face of it. But what they're really thinking, I don't know. A girl like Claire ..."

His voice trailed off and he looked briefly away. Tessa guessed he was probably more upset about this than she was. He had every right to be; after all, he had taught at St David's far longer and would have known Claire better than she did.

"Maybe she's run off with friends. Not girls from the school. Others we don't know about."

Tessa knew she was clutching at the flimsiest of straws.

Mike shrugged. "Possibly. I expect the police will check that out. But from what I know of Claire she didn't have many friends."

"Talking about Claire Marshall, are we?"

Tessa turned round, about to say something sharp. When she saw The Dragon she swallowed the reprimand.

"Don't let it bother you. She's only been gone a day. She'll show up before long I expect, ashamed of herself."

Tessa could hardly believe what she was hearing. But, then again, she should not have expected better of Muriel Neil, the hatchet-faced school head. Her grey hair reflected her personality and the eyes which peered over her half-moon glasses were as hard as steel. Whatever poor Claire Marshall's predicament was, it would earn her no sympathy from The Dragon.

"We don't know that, Miss Neil. She could be – "

"That's right," The Dragon spoke in the kind of tone that indicated end of conversation. "We *don't* know. And until we do know, I suggest we cease to speculate. The children will be upset enough as it is. No need to make it any worse for them."

"We hadn't intended discussing it outside this room," Mike said. "But she's only Year 10. Fourteen years old. When a girl that young disappears without a word it's not good."

"I am perfectly aware of that, thank you very much. But I think it would be better for all concerned if we could put this behind us for now and concentrate on the day ahead."

With that she turned and walked away. Mike's eyes followed her, his face venomous. "Can you believe that old bitch?"

Tessa was spared from having to answer by the sound of the electronic bell rattling out of the staff room speaker. As one the other teachers leapt from their chairs and sofas, pulling their belongings together and making their way to their classrooms. They did not acknowledge her, or Mike. Stuff them, Tessa thought. With the exception of Mike, whose company she appreciated, and Greg, whose company she did not, none of the staff had really spoken to her since her arrival in September. That suited her just fine most of the time, but there were occasions when she felt the need to talk about more than just work, and it was unlikely she would find a friendly listener here. Apart from Mike, not one of them had spoken to her about Claire. If they were going to ignore her about something like that, fat chance they would ever strike up a conversation about something minor. They were too wrapped up in their own little academic world to even consider what was going on outside it.

"I'd better go," Mike said. "You okay?"

"It's not me I'm worried about."

"I didn't mean – "

"Sorry. I know you didn't. It's just … The Dragon and the rest of them. Don't they care about anyone?"

"Other than themselves? Probably not." Mike glanced up at the wall clock. "Anyway, better be off. The kids will be waiting, all ready for their cross-country run. They'll love that."

Tessa appreciated the effort he was making to be upbeat for her sake. "Isn't it a bit cold for cross-country?"

"Got to keep the little buggers from taking up smoking."

Tessa watched him leave, wishing he would stay but knowing that he couldn't and that she would have to move too.

News of Claire's disappearance spread like wildfire. The children were distracted by it, talking and guessing about where she might have gone. Despite Tessa's urging, they got very little work done. The last class before lunch was Claire's own. Tessa felt a flutter of trepidation in her stomach. How would the girl's classmates be taking it? She guessed some of the kids would have created their own scenarios to explain her absence. She had run away to Cardiff or London. She had been kidnapped or, worse, had been murdered, her body dumped in a ditch or in the woods, somewhere where nobody was likely to find it unless by accident.

When the Year 10 class trooped in, however, they were far more subdued that Tessa had expected. Today they were working with watercolours and they set about their tasks promptly, though with little obvious enthusiasm. Now and then one of them would glance at the empty space at the table where Claire normally sat. Sally Jordan in particular, looked close to tears. From the little Tessa knew about them, she was certain the two were fairly close friends. Tessa decided she would have to keep an eye on Sally; if she became upset it would be best to whip her straight out of the art room before the rest of the girls followed suit.

Fortunately the class was not disturbed, other than by a murmur of voices, the occasional nervous laugh and the sound of brushes rattling in jars of water or scraping softly across canvas. When the bell sounded as the clock moved to twelve there was no sudden dash for the door. They washed their brushes and stowed their paintings away slowly, almost as if they were afraid to leave the safety of the room and venture outside, where Claire's disappearance could not easily be kept at arm's length but was a cold, hard reality that they would have to face up to.

Finally they left, Sally Jordan straggling behind. It seemed as if that the girl wanted to say something but could not bring herself to speak. Tessa decided to make the first move for her.

"You okay, Sally?"

The girl's shoulders slumped. Her eyes glistened and she wiped at them, sniffing but not actually crying. "Yeah."

"Sure?"

"I'm sure. I just wish …" Sally dropped her bag and perched on the end of the nearest table. "Claire's never done anything like this before. She's so … so level headed, you know?"

Tessa nodded.

"Like, if ever there's any trouble you know from the start that Claire's the one person who isn't going to be involved. A gang of us went out one night and tried to get served in a pub. Claire wouldn't even come in. She's so straight about things like that."

"You can't think of anywhere she might have gone?"

"No. If I did, I'd tell someone."

"Has she got a boyfriend?"

"Don't think so."

Something about her tone was wrong.

"She never talks about boys?"

Sally glanced over towards the open door, as if making sure no one was eavesdropping. "If I tell you something, do you promise you won't tell anyone else?"

"I can't make a promise like that, Sally. Not if it has a bearing on where Claire might have gone to."

"Okay. But will you promise you won't say who told you?"

"That sounds fair. Come on – what is it?"

Sally hunched forward and her voice lowered. "A couple of weeks back she told me she did have a boyfriend. But she made me swear I wouldn't tell anyone about him. Especially her mother."

"Why not? Girls your age can have boyfriends."

"You don't understand. He's older than her, all right? A lot older. Claire said that if her mum found out, she'd kill her."

"Do you know his name? Or anything else about him? Don't worry, I won't tell anybody you told me but I think this is something I need to pass on. It could be important."

Sally hesitated a moment. Again, Tessa had the impression that the girl was holding something back.

"You're absolutely certain there's nothing else you can think of? It could be very important, Sally."

"Honestly. I only know what I told you. If I … if I think of anything else later, I'll let you know. Okay?"

It wasn't really okay. Tessa was certain there was more to this than Sally was letting on. But it wasn't her place to demand answers. Once the police got around to talking to Claire's friends they could ask her all the questions. Whether Sally decided to answer them was another matter. That wasn't Tessa's business.

"Okay. Off you go, then."

Sally jumped down off the edge of the table and hurried towards the door, like a prisoner released. Just before she left the room she paused and turning back. "Miss - "

"Don't worry," Tessa said with what she hoped was a reassuring smile. "I won't tell anyone you told me."

Alone for the first time since she'd arrived at school that morning, Tessa ran a hand through her hair while she slowly digested what Sally had told her.

She did not like the sound of this. Claire's disappearance was worrying enough in itself. Factor in a boyfriend apparently a lot older than her and it became even more sinister. It was just as well she had not promised to keep it secret. Even if the police didn't ask to speak to her, this was something she should volunteer. Or was it? Claire was a teenage girl and teenage girls like to make up stories to impress their friends. Maybe that's all this mysterious boyfriend was; a concoction born of an immature mind to help a teenage girl try to lead the others in the cool stakes. Listening to them talk, all teenage girls had boyfriends. Maybe Claire was insecure enough to try to stay one step ahead of the pack by making out that hers was not a boyfriend but a *man* friend.

Maybe by telling the police, all Tessa would be doing was muddying the waters, adding complications to their investigation when no such complications existed. For all she knew Claire had, for whatever reason, simply run away. Maybe she had crashed out on some hitherto unknown friend's floor as the result of a family spat; would eventually get in touch with her mother to let her know she was safe and well, just as soon as she'd cooled down.

On the other hand, maybe there was a boyfriend.

And maybe Claire had run off with him.

In which case Tessa had to tell the police. There was no telling what an older man's intentions might be.

Shit.

No point trying to decide what to do about it now. She had more classes this afternoon, younger pupils who would demand all her attention. It would be better, she felt, to wait until her mind was clear and then she could think how best to use the information.

The day wore on. Outside, the January sky darkened. Looking out of the window, Tessa thought she saw the odd wisp of snow drift to the ground. On days like this she kept a regular eye on the weather; should it really start to fall she would have to leave early. The main road from Builth Wells was usually kept clear, but the side road to Bethesda tended to remain untreated. That was all she needed, to be stuck in her car a few miles from the cottage during the first blizzard of the year.

When the art room emptied for the last time that day, she felt a sudden sense of relief. A few of the kids had asked her about Claire and she had done her best to reassure them. Now at last she could head off home and stop pretending. That was what she had been doing all day; pretending that everything would turn out all right, because the alternative did not even bear contemplating. Tessa closed her eyes and massaged them, as if trying to rub the memory of Claire's pretty face from her mind.

She rinsed brushes in the sink. Normally she would have made the kids clean them before they left, but this time she allowed them to leave their mess behind, so anxious was she to have a little time to herself.

"You okay?"

The voice from behind made her jump. Dirty grey water splashed over her jeans and she muttered a curse.

"Sorry." It was Mike Jenkins. "Didn't mean to startle you."

"Don't worry. It's only water. It'll dry."

"But won't the paint - ?"

"Mike, forget it. Were you after anything?"

"No, no, nothing in particular. Just making sure you were okay. It's been a pretty tense day for all of us."

Tessa dropped the remaining dirty brushes back into the water; they could wait until the morning. She leaned against the sink edge while she dried her hands on a paper towel. "I don't suppose there's been any word. From Claire's mother."

"Nothing. She must be frantic with worry."

"I can't imagine what she's really going through. I doubt anyone could, unless it's happened to them."

"God forbid. Well, anyway, as long as you're okay … "

"I'm fine. Thanks for your concern, by the way. I mean it."

And she did. Just before Christmas she had felt that Mike was steeling himself to ask her out. And she had hoped like hell that he wouldn't. She liked him, found him charming and – yes, she had to admit it – physically attractive. But she wasn't ready for a man, not yet. The last thing she would have wanted was to upset Mike and risk losing the closest thing she had to a friend in the life she had chosen for herself. Fortunately he had never asked.

"See you tomorrow," he said and, giving her a farewell wink, left her alone once more.

The pain was intense. She felt like she was being burnt alive. Smoke choked her. She panicked; a fire. Suddenly the heat was gone, replaced with a cold so deep that it snatched her breath away. She gasped and icy water poured into her mouth and lungs. She tried to move but she was frozen. No – she felt a pressure on her shoulders. She was being held down. Her eyes saw only brightness, wavering as though glimpsed through a swirling current. Beyond the light was shadow. It moved, drawing closer.

Then darkness encroached on the edges of her vision, swiftly growing inwards until she could see no more ...

Tuesday passed slowly. The tension in the air was almost tangible. There had been no news about Claire. Worse, the police had been in touch; they wanted to arrange interviews with the staff and the kids in the missing girl's class.

All along Tessa had been certain that Claire had run off, with or without a boyfriend, and that sooner or later she would call or turn up at home. But now that the police were coming into the school, it seemed they were bringing a harsher truth with them. She tried to remain optimistic but it was not easy. Every hour that passed felt like another nail in the girl's coffin.

Tessa shook her head, angry with herself.

Claire was fine. There was no other way of looking at it.

The children went through the motions during her classes. There was no enthusiasm, no laughter, no joy in the act of expressing themselves through art. Neither was Tessa able to summon the enthusiasm to try to shake them out of their torpor. She could not stop thinking about Claire, and about Sally's revelation. And when she wasn't turning the story over in her mind, she found herself contemplating last night's dream.

It could not be ignored.

Her dreams always meant something.

That was something she had learned the hard way.

The trouble was, they were not always literal. Sometimes the images her mind conjured while she slept were more like pointers towards the truth. Figuring them out, interpreting those visual hieroglyphics was always the challenge. The first dream had, she felt, been about drowning in icy water. Last night, though, it had felt like she was burning and *then* drowning. What the hell that was supposed to mean was anyone's guess.

Tessa had no fear of water; she was a strong swimmer. So was her subconscious trying to warn her of a fire, possibly in her home? There was always a chance, of course, but Tessa had paid for the place to be completely rewired before moving in and there were smoke detectors on both floors.

Besides, even if the dream was a foretelling of fire, why would she then feel like she was drowning in icy water?

It made no sense.

At last the bell rang. The children walked disconsolately out of the room; the fact that they were going home was not enough to raise their spirits. Tessa smiled at them as they departed, trying to convey the impression of normality that she knew they could see right through. If this was what they were like now, what would they be like when the police started asking questions?

Speaking of the police, Tessa knew she really should tell them about Sally's story. Sure, she could wait a day or two until they came into school. But what if, by putting it off until then, Tessa only made Claire's situation more serious? Worst of all – and she knew she was getting melodramatic here yet couldn't help it – what if the delay had meant the difference between life and death?

You should have told them yesterday. You'll still have to explain why you waited 24 hours. You knew it was important.

Not necessarily. She wouldn't have to say when she found out about the mystery boyfriend.

Yes, but you'll know, won't you?

You'll have to live with the guilt if it all goes wrong.

Tessa cursed her own stupid indecisiveness.

She pictured herself facing Claire's mother if worse came to worst, knowing she could have saved her daughter.

Claire's mother.

Tessa pondered this a moment before reaching a decision. She left the art room, locking the door behind her, and made her way along the empty corridors to the school office. It would take her only a matter of minutes to look up Claire's address. Then she would pay a call on the way home. While she was at it, she would tell Mrs Mitchell what she had learned, knowing that in turn the child's mother would immediately pass that information on to the police, just as Tessa should have done in the first place.

She felt rotten; a coward. But the damage had been done now and at least she was trying to put it right. After all, she could have said nothing, could have dismissed it as nothing more than a teenage girl's fantasy which was not worth repeating.

It was almost dark by the time she left St David's. The warmth of the school evaporated the second she walked out of the door, and freezing January air assailed her. Tessa tugged her fleece collar up and hurried across to the car park, the frosty ground crunching under her feet. She glanced nervously skywards and was dismayed at the sight of so many low, grey clouds. So far that day the weather had remained clear but it looked like that would not last for long.

It had taken longer than she'd expected to dig out Claire's file. By the time she had found it the rest of the school had emptied. Now her battered old Escort was the only vehicle left in the car park. Tessa felt a vague apprehension as she approached it; no doubt a hangover of the grim mood in school all day. She looked around nervously, for a moment convinced there was someone else nearby. As far as she could see, though, she was the only living soul around.

She drove out of town and on to the A-road that led back to Bethesda, squinting to see through the glass which had turned almost opaque despite the attentions of the heater and her own wiping hand. Gradually, as the miles ticked by, the air inside the car grew noticeably warmer and the view ahead cleared. The Escort's headlights picked out the black surface of the road and the blurred white streaks of the lane markings. Outside this illuminated cone there was an impenetrable darkness. Not for the first time since winter had sent in, Tessa felt as if she was driving through an endless tunnel. The sight of headlamps heading towards her always brought with it a flicker of comfort. It meant she was not alone, something that was quite easy to forget out here.

Hebron was not far from Bethesda. In fact, Tessa knew that, half-way round the lake, there was another forest path leading down to the village, though she had never walked it.

It was a small place; not too many houses, a country pub with an old-fashioned swinging sign that proclaimed it to be the Fox and Hounds, and a small store that fulfilled the functions of grocer, newsagents and post office. Side roads led off the main drive through. Tessa cruised past them, scanning the signs. Finally she saw it; Beacons View. Nerves fluttered in her stomach as she guided the Escort along the narrow street, passing a row of detached bungalows. These gave way to larger houses. All had neat gardens and most had two cars on the driveway. It did not take a genius to figure out that there was serious money here.

Tessa spotted number thirty-three and pulled up outside it, next to a grey Volvo that looked curiously out of place in such affluent surroundings; no doubt her Escort did too.

She reached out to open the door, wanting to get this over with as quickly as possible. But her fingers seemed frozen to the handle. It was so tempting to start the car up again and hit the road to Bethesda. The prospect of facing Claire's mother – hell, for all Tessa knew there could be a whole houseful of relatives in there with her, helping her through her ordeal – was such a daunting one that she had serious doubts she could go through with it. She was a teacher, not a social worker. She would not know where to start.

Right then an image of Claire's smiling face, framed by a mass of wavy blonde hair, sprung to mind and she knew that, like it or not, this was something she could not turn away from.

As she was locking the car door she heard a noise from behind her and, turning around, saw that the Volvo's side window had been wound down. A middle-aged man nodded at her, then towards the Marshall house. "You headed there?" A cloud of mist flavoured with cigarette smoke escaped from his mouth when he spoke. "That is, if you don't mind me asking."

Claire wasn't sure whether she should answer; the man could be anyone. Courtesy prevailed and she nodded.

"She's not talking, you know."

"Sorry?"

"The kid's mother. No interviews, no pics, nothing. Police put out a mis per report this morning but she ain't co-operating."

"Mis per?"

"Missing person." The journalist, presumably from one of the local weeklies as it was doubtful the nationals would have picked up the story yet, threw his cigarette end through the open window. It glowed brightly on the pavement. "You police or press?"

"Neither. I'm ... a family friend."

Tessa almost let slip that she was Claire's teacher, but bit the words back just in time. The last thing she wanted was to be pestered for an interview. She didn't want to be there at all.

"Well, would you do us a favour and ask her if she'll change her mind about talking? Tell her it could help."

Sure. And I bet that's what they always say.

"I'll ask," she assured the reporter. "But I doubt she'll change her mind. I wouldn't, if it was my daughter."

"Neither would I if it was mine."

He nodded and wound the window back up. An orange glow lit up the Volvo interior; another cigarette already. Tessa guessed he was there for the duration. She didn't envy him.

It was a solid redbrick house, a good age but well maintained, with brown framed double-glazed windows and doors that enhanced the impression of class. The curtains were pulled but Tessa could see a soft light behind them. There was no car parked outside but as there was a detached garage to the side of the house that did not mean anything. A part of her wanted Claire's mother to be out. Another part hoped she was in.

She rapped with gloved knuckles on the front door and tried to think of what she was going to say when, or if, she had an answer. There was no point trying to pretend she was there for any reason other than the fact that Claire was missing.

A light went on in the hallway.

Then a silhouette appeared behind the door glass, growing larger as it drew nearer. A safety chain rattled and then the door swung inwards an inch or two, barely sufficient for her to make out a pinched white face. "Yes?"

"Mrs Marshall?"

"I'm sorry. I have nothing to say – "

She began to close the door.

Tessa instinctively put her hand against it. "Wait, please. I'm not from the papers. I'm Tessa James – Claire's art teacher."

There was a momentary pause during which the door seemed frozen into place. Then it opened wide and a tall, slim woman, as dark as her daughter was fair, ushered her in. "Sorry about the welcome," she said as she pushed the door shut against the frigid evening air. "I've had two reporters on the phone and another at the door."

"I know. I just saw him."

Tessa wiped her boots on a mat just inside the hall, and then followed her host into a large sitting room. In other circumstances Mrs Marshall would no doubt be just as attractive as her daughter. Now, though, the flesh beneath her eyes seemed bruised by worry and her slender body was slightly stooped, as though bowing under the pressure. A lack of make-up made her skin appear deathly pale and her black hair hung lank and unwashed.

"I didn't catch your name," she said, lowering herself into a chair and indicating that Tessa should sit on the sofa opposite.

"It's Tessa. Tessa James. Mrs Marshall – "

"Please. Call me Chris."

"Chris. I want you to know I'm so sorry about what has happened. If there's anything I can do to help, just say it."

Anything except find her for you, that is.

"I appreciate the offer but," and here her eyes darted to the phone which sat on a small table in the corner, "there's nothing much that *can* be done. All I can do is wait for her to call."

They sat in awkward silence for a moment or two. Tessa, now feeling the heat, unzipped her fleece and took off her gloves, stuffing them into one pocket. Having made the journey here, she was annoyed with herself for not being able to think of a single thing to say. The only words that came to mind were banal, meaningless platitudes.

There's been no word at all? How awful for you.

If that was the best she could come up with, she might just as well have gone straight home.

"You're new, aren't you?"

"Sorry?"

"At the school, I mean. I seem to recall Claire talking about a new art teacher. She seemed quite taken with you."

Tessa shifted uncomfortably. She was already feeling guilty enough. Still, she was glad that Mrs Marshall had managed to find a way to break the silence where she had so dismally failed.

"She's a good kid. Very talented. She has a natural eye for shape and colour."

Chris Marshall smiled a little wistfully. "Claire has always loved drawing, ever since she was little. She had a crayon in her hand the moment she was old enough to hold one. She spends half her life up in her room, you know, working away."

Tessa sat forward. "Working on what?"

"Her pictures. She loves to sit on her bed with a pad and pencil and dream up all these wonderful portraits and scenes."

Whether it was a deliberate show of optimism or just force of habit, her use of the present tense did not escape Tessa.

In fact she was surprised at how talkative Mrs Marshall was, given what she must be feeling. Or maybe she was grasping the opportunity to open up, grateful for the company. Tessa had no idea if there was a Mr Marshall, or if Claire was an only child. She had heard no sounds from the rest of the house, save for the soft rush of water in the radiators and the occasional muted thump from the central heating boiler. If Chris Marshall was a single mother – which, thinking about it, would make her ordeal all the more dreadful – then she either had a great job or had been left a substantial amount of money. Tessa could only dream of owning a house like this. The living room alone was almost as big as the entire ground floor of her cottage; every fixture and fitting looked like it had cost a small fortune. Not that Tessa was envious. She guessed that Chris Marshall would happily give it all away to have her daughter back.

"Do you want to see some of her pictures?"

"Yes. I'd like that."

"You might as well come up to her bedroom," Mrs Marshall said, rising from the chair. "No point dragging them all down."

"I don't want to put you to any trouble."

"It's no trouble. You're Claire's art teacher, after all. I think they're excellent, but then I would. I'd like your opinion."

She led Tessa out into the hallway, and then up steep, carpeted stairs to the first floor. As she stepped into Claire's room Tessa's eyes were immediately drawn to the array of pop posters on the wall. Busted. Justin Timberlake. Some boy band that she did not recognise but whose five members looked like school kids trying their best to pretend they were James Dean. A single bed ran along one wall, flanked by a small dressing table. Bookshelves and a double wardrobe covered the other wall. The large window revealed nothing but Tessa and Chris Marshall's ghosts, haunting a brightly-lit mirror image of the bedroom.

Tessa looked away. The darkness bothered her.

"Make yourself comfortable."

There were no seats, so Tessa perched on the side of the bed while Claire's mother reached under it, removing a thick stack of papers. "Here," she said, holding them out.

Tessa took them off her and rested them on her lap. Of course she was going to praise them, no matter how amateurish they may be. Claire was only fourteen, after all. And while she did have a natural talent, it was raw and unfocused. But when Tessa began flicking through the pictures, she was quickly forced to revise her opinion.

Claire working alone at home was a better artist by far than Claire working in school, surrounded by others. It was as if, here in the sanctuary of her bedroom, she felt sufficiently confident to express herself in ways she would never have dared in class.

Some were no more than small pencil sketches while others were larger mixed medium landscape using all combination of watercolour, pencil and gouache. They were stunning.

She glanced up, about to say what she thought, swallowing the words when she saw that Mrs Marshall was gazing through the window, a faraway look in her eyes. Tessa wondered what was going through her mind. Was she seeing in the darkness an image of her daughter, alive and waiting for the right moment to call home? Or seeing her body, lifeless and broken, dumped in some secret place where it might never be found other than by chance?

She was jarred from her thought by the ringing of a telephone from downstairs. Chris Marshall visibly jumped at the sound of it. She pushed herself off the bed. "Excuse me," she said as she hurried out of the room. "It might be …"

Her words faded into silence as she hurried to the door. Tessa nodded her understanding but by then the woman was already dashing down the stairs. The ringing continued for several more moments and then abruptly stopped. Tessa hoped its cessation was because Mrs Marshall had answered, rather than because the caller had given up waiting. She strained to listen but there was nothing. Her stomach felt like it had tied itself up in knots. At last she heard a voice from below, too low to be audible. Tessa prayed it was good news; or, if not good then at least not bad. Surely, though, if the unthinkable had happened the police would have turned up in person. There was nothing Tessa could do other than wait, chewing her lip nervously and dreading the moment when she heard footsteps climbing the stairs.

To distract herself she eased herself off the mattress and wandered over to the bookcase. Row after row of paperback spines faced her. Stephen King. Harry Potter. At one end of the highest shelf, much larger than the books that leaned against it, was a lavish hardback of The Lord of the Rings. Tessa reached up, took it down and opened it. She saw it was illustrated with full colour plates by Alan Lee, whose work she admired. She spent a minute or two immersed in Lee's stunning visualisation of Middle Earth then, feeling slightly guilty that she had momentarily forgotten where she was, lifted up the book to put it back.

It would not sit flush with the back of the bookcase.

Tessa frowned. It was important to her that she should leave the room exactly as she had found it. She pulled the Tolkien out again and reached up for the empty space, trying to discover what was in the way, assuming that one of the paperbacks had toppled over. Her hand, however, closed on a slim hardback. Tessa took it from the shelf. It was, she saw, a diary.

She told me she did have a boyfriend.

Tessa recalled what Sally had told her.

She made me swear I wouldn't tell anyone about him.

Claire had her secrets, like any teenage girl.

Sometimes teenage girls told their diaries secrets that they would never share with anyone, not even their closest friends.

Especially her mother.

Tessa came close to putting it back, unread. It was none of her business. If there was anything within its pages that did point to the identity of this mysterious boyfriend then surely it was for Claire's mother to discover, not her. Yet, despite this, she found she could not let it go. Realising there was no point even trying to justify it – she simply had to know – she opened the book and flicked randomly through it. The initial entries were typical teenage notes, probably much like the ones Tessa would have written in her own diary, if she could remember that far back. It was all innocent, inconsequential stuff about school and home and CDs she had bought or wanted to buy.

Then an entry caught Tessa's eye.

I saw him tonight. He pulled up in his car when I was walking back from the shop and offered me a lift in his car. I said no. It wasn't far and anyway someone might see us. They all gossip round here. I didn't want to get into trouble.

Heart racing slightly, Tessa turned page after page, searching for mentions of this unidentified man.

I dreamt about him last night. Dreamt he was kissing me, touching me in places he wasn't supposed to. I knew it was wrong but I didn't want it to stop. I know it's crazy but I think I'm in love with him. For real, that is. Not in the dream. Stupid, stupid.

The reference to dreams struck a chord. Tessa knew not to dismiss them. But had Claire felt the same way? Or was the dream itself nothing more than a fiction, conjured by a mixed-up young girl who liked reading fantasy novels?

Knowing there was every chance that Chris Marshall could return to the room at any moment, Tessa flicked through the pages more quickly. She stopped at another entry. Like its predecessors it was not dated; she had no way of telling how long had passed since Claire's apparent dream. It could have been days or months.

I must be mad. If they find out about us then we'll both be in really deep shit. He'll lose his job, everything. And the police will have him, because I'm under age. But he says he doesn't care and neither do I. We love each other. We always will.

Tessa closed her eyes briefly, shaken by pity and anger.

The poor kid. Whoever this bastard was, he had known how to use her emotions against her

Then she found a few brief sentences penned in a barely legible scrawl rather than Claire's normally meticulous handwriting.

He's trying to persuade me go with him. He won't say where. I don't like it. But I don't know what to do. I can't tell anyone. I daren't. I know what he'd do if our secret got out.

Tessa swallowed. She realised her hands were sweating and she put the diary down long enough to wipe them dry on her jeans.

Then she picked up the book again, turning to the final entry.

I told him I thought we should stop seeing each other and he went mad. I've never seen him so angry. He said that if he couldn't have me he'd make sure nobody else could. Then he laughed and he said he was only joking but I knew he wasn't. I can't tell anyone about him. I'm afraid of what he'll do to me if anyone finds out about us or if I try to leave him. I don't know what to do.

Tessa closed the diary. She could read no more. Had Claire been crying as she wrote those last few dozen words? Or had her hands been trembling with a fear that she was desperately trying not to show to her mother? Tessa felt chilled by the helpless tone of the girl's words, which cast a sinister new light over her disappearance. It now seemed unlikely that Claire had merely absconded with an older man with whom she was besotted; but not unreasonable to assume she had been taken against her will.

There was another, even darker, possibility which Tessa refused to dwell on. Dear God, she was worried enough already. Guilt wracked her again when she remembered she could have told the police about Claire's anonymous boyfriend yesterday. Her only consolation was the thought that she would only have been passing on hearsay. Now, however, she had solid proof to show that he did indeed exist and had threatened Claire at least once.

"You like books?"

Tessa started violently. She hadn't heard Chris Marshall come back up the stairs.

"Sorry. I didn't mean to make you jump."

Tessa held the diary loosely at her side. She knew she had to hand it over and was desperately trying to pluck up the courage.

"Was it anything important - the phone call?"

She knew it had not been about Claire; her mother was too calm. But she had to ask, anyway.

Mrs Marshall pulled a face. "Only my ex. Calls every few hours to see if there's any news. Keeps asking if he can come over and stay until Claire shows up, but I told him no."

"I take it you didn't part on the best of terms."

"You could say that."

"I know how you feel." Tessa held the book out, before her nerve failed her. "I think you'd better see this."

"What is it?"

"Claire's diary. It was hidden in the bookcase. I found it by accident while I was looking at one of her books."

Mrs Marshall frowned as she turned the diary over, then back again. "Funny. Claire never mentioned this. Not once."

She started to open it.

Tessa said: "I think you'd better sit down, Chris."

"Why?" Her tone was more confused than hostile.

"Did you know Claire had a boyfriend?"

Chris Marshall stared at her a moment, mouth an O of surprise, then she shook her head. "Claire's got a one or two friends who are boys, if that's what you mean."

"It's not what I mean." Tessa swallowed. She would give anything not to be there right then. "I'm sorry to have to tell you this, but Claire could be in a lot of trouble."

Mrs Marshall went to say something. Tessa raised a hand, cutting her off before she could start.

"Let me finish, okay? I heard a couple of kids talking in the corridor today." The lie tripped off her tongue effortlessly, allowing her to neatly sidestep a potential confrontation. "They reckoned Claire had been seeing someone ... an older man."

Now Mrs Marshall did sound hostile. "Is this supposed to be funny? Do you have any idea what I'm going through – "

"Read the diary, Chris."

"It's just gossip. You know how kids make up stories."

"Chris. Read it."

For a moment she thought Mrs Marshall was going to hurl the diary at her, she looked that angry. Instead the other woman threw Tessa a baleful glance and opened the slender book, bending its cover back so sharply that the spine creaked, threatening to break. Tessa stood at the bookcase, not daring to move, watching as Chris Marshall sat on the edge of the bed and began to read. For several long minutes there was silence, except for the rustle of pages being turned. Then Tessa saw Mrs Marshall's brows furrow and she drew in breath sharply. What little colour there had been in her face seemed to drain away.

When she looked up her eyes were filled with despair. Tessa found herself aching with pity.

"Do you have any idea who this ... this man is?"

Tessa shook her head. "No. I just overheard a conversation between a few kids. I didn't take it seriously."

Mrs Marshall ran a hand over her face and sighed deeply. For a moment Tessa thought she was going to burst into tears. But she must been able to draw on some inner reserve of strength, for she almost leapt up off the mattress, holding the diary aloft like a trophy. "I have to call the police and tell them about this."

She walked quickly out of the room, Tessa close behind.

At the bottom of the stairs she reached out and touched Mrs Marshall's shoulder. The woman halted and turned round sharply.

"Do you want me to stay? I would imagine the police will send someone out tonight. I can wait with you, if you like."

Chris Marshall stared at her with an expression that could have been suspicion or doubt. Then her face softened. "That's very kind of you, but I think I'd rather deal with this on my own."

"Honestly, I don't mind."

"I'll be fine. And I'm touched that you took the time to call to see me. You're the first from the school to visit, you know."

Tessa didn't know. The Dragon really was an uncaring bitch.

"It was the least I could do." Tessa felt as if she should say more before she left. A few telling words, something that Mrs Marshall might remember and draw comfort from when her spirits were at their lowest. But her mind remained stubbornly blank.

"You go and make your phone call. I'll see myself out."

"Okay. And thank you again."

Tessa put her hand on the lock to open it, but then thought of something that she *could* do. She reached into her fleece pocket and pulled out a card. "Take this," she said, handing it to Mrs Marshall. "It's got all my numbers on it; home, school and mobile. If there's any news about Claire or anything I can do, just call."

For a moment Mrs Marshall looked close to tears. "I will."

Claire reached out and touched the woman's arm lightly. "I'm sure everything's going to turn out all right. Just be strong."

She did not wait for a response. Instead she turned the lock and opened the door, pulling it shut behind her as she hurried out into the cold, uncaring night. Her footsteps echoed around the street as she walked quickly down the path. The reporter's car had disappeared; doubtless he had realised he was wasting his time and had decided to cut his losses. Tessa supposed, with a pang of dismay, that he would have a better story to chase in the morning.

That was, of course, unless Claire called in the meantime.

As much as she hoped that would happen, Tessa had to admit that it was more plausible that, come tomorrow, nothing would have changed except for the urgency of the search.

The air was so cold it made her hands and face hurt. Tessa pulled out her gloves and struggled with numb fingers to get them on. Clouds had kept the ice at bay so the Escort's windscreen was mercifully clear; she would not have to spend time having to scrape it down. She unlocked the door and got in, shivering, looking forward to the moment when she reached the cottage and could relax with a cup of tea while her evening meal was cooking. She started the engine and turned the heater on, glad that the air in the car was still fairly warm.

She had to wait at the junction. A huge lorry crawled along the main road, leading a procession of cars. Tessa pulled the handbrake on, mentally urging them to get out of her way so she could start moving again. At least they were going in the opposite direction to her; being stuck behind that slow-moving cavalcade would have been torture. Finally the last car crept past.

The Escort's lights caught it fully side-on.

Tessa saw Greg Roberts, sitting behind the wheel.

As he passed by he turned and looked straight at her.

She was burning. Her lungs were clogged with smoke. She tried to scream but no words came out. And then there was no heat, only cold; a fierce, bone-penetrating chill so intense that it burned as much as the fire. Again she tried to call out but liquid ice poured down her throat. A rushing sound filled her ears and she knew she was under water. She began to struggle as her body cried out for air, but she could not move. There was a weight on her shoulders which she fought against. Yet no matter how violently she thrashed about she could not free herself from the force that held her under. Her struggles weakened as the last of the air in her lungs slowly leaked away. Suddenly the pressure on her shoulders relaxed but even then she could not move. There was light above her and, beyond it, a shadow which loomed closer until she could discern the distorted outline of a human figure. Just before she drifted slowly into everlasting darkness the last two words she would ever think blazed in her mind like a fire in the night sky. My killer.

Tessa gasped as she opened her eyes. Her body was drenched in sweat and the raw air of the room brushed her skin with chilly fingers. When she reached down to pull up the quilt she found she must have kicked it off while she slept. She looked at the clock. Just after four. Too early for the central heating; no wonder she was cold. She groaned and reached one hand to the floor, seized the edge of the quilt and tugged it back on the bed, wrapping it tightly around herself until she began to feel warm again.

She closed her eyes and tried to get back to sleep, but it was useless. The dream haunted her waking moments as surely as it haunted her sleep. Until now it had been like watching a film repeatedly, a film that re-edited itself every time it was shown so that the overall story was the same but individual scenes were played out in subtly different ways.

Now, though, the film had been extended.

My killer.

Tessa shook her head as if that would banish the words from her mind. They refused to be erased. She pushed herself up on one elbow to switch on the bedside lamp, closing her eyes against the sudden burst of light. Her stomach felt as if something unpleasant were crawling around inside it.

She had been burning and then she had been drowning.

Someone had held her down in the water until she died.

She had not seen his face but she knew who he was.

My killer.

Surely it could not be coincidence. The dreams had started the night before she had found out about Claire going missing.

Tessa ran a hand over her face, feeling slightly sick.

There was always the chance that her dream had been coloured by what she had read in Claire's diary, but she did not think so. It had felt absolutely real; she could still feel the cold of the water in her mouth, could smell the smoke from the burning.

It had happened like this once before, with Molly Danvers.

Tessa had been so convinced the dream about Molly was real that she'd acted on it, and her hunch had paid off. Admittedly she had failed to prevent the accident but she had been there within minutes and tending to Molly while the ambulance arrived.

This dream felt as real as the one about Molly.

But what the hell could she do this time?

Telling Chris Marshall about Claire's boyfriend was one thing. Calling the police to tell them that she'd dreamed that the girl was dead — murdered – was asking for trouble. They would either dismiss her as a sick hoaxer or arrest her for wasting police time.

Not that she would blame them. If someone else had told Tessa they had dreamed about Claire's murder she would not have believed them, either.

She didn't want to believe it now. Except she was horribly certain she was right. And the worst of it was that she knew she would have to keep the knowledge to herself. There was no one else she trusted enough to confide her fears in, not even Mike Jenkins. He was a nice enough guy but they were not so close for her to feel comfortable talking to him about anything like this. Tessa felt a great welling of sorrow. There was no longer any doubt in her mind that Claire was dead.

Whatever the dreams had been trying to tell her, it was too late to save the girl.

Maybe it had always been too late. For all she knew, Claire had been murdered on Sunday. Tessa sat up, mind awhirl. What if the dream had not been intended to prevent the murder but something else entirely? There had been someone leaning over her – Claire – as she lay dying in the water. If Tessa dreamed the dream again and it continued to reinvent itself, would the face of the killer ultimately be revealed to her?

Was that the purpose of the dream - not to save her life but to bring a murderer to justice?

Tessa slumped back on the bed, too tired to think straight, let alone try to second-guess the unknown.

Maybe the dream was no more than that; a dream.

She switched the lamp off, yawning widely, and then settled back under the quilt. Tomorrow she would ponder the implications of the dream further.

A thought nagged at the back of her mind but Tessa chose to ignore it. She was shattered. If she didn't at least try to get back to sleep now she would be sorry when the alarm went off.

Soon she slept. If she dreamed, she remembered nothing of it in the morning.

It was snowing when she left the cottage. A strong wind made the flurries twist and twirl, keeping the road fairly clear but creating drifts against walls and in sheltered corners. Tessa wondered if she was making the right decision by going to school rather than staying at home and avoiding the prospect of being stranded. But she was not comfortable with the idea of being alone. Even if the staff were not good company, the kids were. It was almost as if, by being around them, she could draw on their youthfulness to boost her own flagging vitality. Besides, if the weather took a turn for the worse she would leave early. The Dragon would probably have something to say about that, but she could go to hell.

Tessa could not believe the old cow had not called on Chris Marshall. How could someone be that uncaring?

She arrived with ten minutes to spare and went directly to the staff room, needing coffee for warmth and to clear her head. Bill Murphy, the crusty old head of religious studies, gave her a grim-faced nod as she walked in. The other half-dozen or so, sitting around in small groups, did not even offer that small token of acknowledgement. Tessa felt like a ghost.

As she waited at the machine for her coffee, the door banged open and Greg Roberts slouched in. His hair, normally gelled into place, was no longer slicked back but sticking out in tufts at all angles, like a middle-aged punk. Tessa guessed he had worn a hat to combat the blustery snowstorm and was now paying the price. He removed his misted-up glasses and squinted around the room while he polished them on his tie. Putting them back on, he looked at Tessa and began to pick his way towards her.

Shit.

Where was Mike Jenkins when she needed rescuing?

"Get you a coffee?"

Tessa lifted her cup from the dispenser. "You're too late."

"Maybe next time, eh?"

She started to edge away from him, feeling slightly repulsed by his presence. As usual she had the impression he was mentally undressing her. "Is there any news on that missing kid? Claire whatever-her-name-is?"

"You mean Claire Marshall?"

Tessa did not particularly want to talk about it; not to Greg Roberts in any event. Last night's dream still bothered her. Once again she was struck by an overwhelming certainty that the girl would never be coming home; that she was dead and her killer was still out there.

"No," she said. "No news that I'm aware of."

"Well, no point in worrying. There's nothing we can do about it. Now then, when are we going to have that badminton match?"

Tessa felt herself slump. Would he ever take the hint?

"Not while the weather's this bad. I don't fancy getting stuck in the school hall if we stay on to play."

"There's a pretty goods sports centre in Llanelwed. Only five minutes from the house. Plenty of room if you want to stay over."

Christ, he was insistent. And Tessa would rather spend the night naked in a frozen field than in his house.

"Thanks for the offer," she said, forcing the words out. "But I don't like leaving the cottage empty when it's this cold. Not when there's a risk of frozen pipes."

It sounded pathetic even to her ears. Roberts stared at her for a moment, his lips curled into the sneer that passed for a smile. Tessa did not like the look in his eyes, as if he had not only seen through her story but was making sure she knew that he had.

Then he shrugged. "Fair enough. Another time, eh?"

The bell sounded, rescuing her from the obligation to respond.

"Got to go," she said, tossing the remains of her coffee into the sink and dropping the plastic cup into the bin. She left without looking to see if Roberts was behind her; his classroom was in a different direction to hers, so there was no reason why he should be. Kids bustled past her, hurrying to the main hall. Assembly and registration would take maybe half an hour, giving Tessa plenty of time to get the art room ready for them.

The corridor was suddenly quiet. Tessa glanced back over her shoulder, feeling stupid for sensing that Greg Roberts really had decided to follow her. There was something about him, a kind of slimy oiliness that chilled her insides. And he was not just a letch but a persistent one at that. She had the terrible feeling he would just keep on pestering until she gave in, and that was something she could never bring herself to do. Christ, for him to invite her to his house was beyond belief.

Tessa slowed her pace as a thought occurred to her.

Roberts had said that he lived in Llanelwed.

The place was on the other side of Builth Wells from Bethesda. How come, then, that she had seen him in Hebron last night? It was hardly an evening for a scenic drive.

He had appeared to look straight at her.

Yet he could not have been; with the Escort's headlights dazzling him there was no way he could have recognised Tessa.

Which meant it was Beacons View he had been staring at.

Well, of course he would have been. Claire lived there and everyone in the school knew what had happened. It would have been only natural for him to glance at it as he drove by.

Or would it?

Only minutes earlier Roberts had appeared to have had difficulty recalling the girl's name. If that were the case, if he had not merely been feigning indifference for whatever misguided reason, was it likely he would have known where she lived?

Tessa chewed on her lip, not liking the path that her thinking appeared to following.

Greg Roberts had an eye not just for the ladies but for the young girls too. Tessa recalled the predatory glance he had given the group who had overtaken them in the yard the other morning. Had he had moved up from just lecherous stares? Had he seen Claire Marshall one night and offered her a lift home? And had she naively accepted, looking on him as nothing more than a thoughtful teacher offering her a lift for safety's sake?

It could have started out innocently enough, from Claire's perspective at least, and then developed into something more sinister. Tessa understood why some pupils were drawn to their teachers. More often than not it had nothing to do with physical attraction and more a feeling of being close to a source of power.

Greg. Pompous and self-opinionated Greg, struck her as the type of man who revelled in being in such a position of authority.

Tessa shook her head, surprised at how seriously she was beginning to take this. It was idle speculation with no evidence other than the most loosely circumstantial to back it up.

Still. It *was* possible.

She reached the art room and unlocked it, then pottered around inside. Ostensibly she was getting the place ready for lessons but in truth her mind was far away, mulling over scenario after scenario to explain Claire's disappearance, but always reaching the same conclusion.

Claire had written in her diary that if anyone found out about them her boyfriend would lose his job, or worse.

Greg Roberts could have broken what was, for a teacher, the ultimate taboo; an emotional – maybe a physical – relationship with a pupil. It did not happen as frequently as most people imagined; the stakes were too high.

Some of them, though, were prepared to risk it.

Was Greg, as unattractive as Tessa found him, desperate enough to risk throwing his life down the pan?

The girl had also written that the boyfriend was trying to persuade her to go with him. He would not say where.

Greg, she knew all too well, was not only persistent but insidious. It did not take much of a leap of imagination to picture him worming his way into a young girl's affections. And he had invited Tessa to his house and would quite probably continue to ask. Had that been where he was planning to take Claire?

But assuming she had interpreted her dreams correctly, Claire was dead. Murdered, presumably by this mystery boyfriend who had made veiled threats about what he would do to her if she ever told anyone about him, or tried to leave him.

She could just about picture Greg Roberts breaking that great taboo and starting a relationship with an under-age girl. Try as she might, however, she could not picture him killing her. Not unless he had a dark side that he kept well hidden.

Or Claire really had intended to end or expose their relationship and he had killed her in the heat of the moment.

Children arrived, pouring into the classroom with a sudden burst of sound; voices, chairs being dragged back, the clatter of art materials being dropped casually onto tables. Tessa pushed her thoughts to one side and forced herself to concentrate on the task at hand. No matter how much it all seemed to add up, there was nothing she could do about it. There was no way she could make an accusation like that against Greg or anyone else, not without a shred of evidence to support it.

She could not even voice her suspicions to another member of staff. Back in London many of her colleagues had also been friends; she could have confided in them knowing the conversation would not be repeated. Here she had no such luxury. Chances were she'd be out of a job before she knew what was happening.

Lunch times were mainly spent in solitude. If the weather was nice Tessa normally strolled into Builth, not for the shops but just to get out of school. Today, though, that was out of the question. She ate in the dining room, on a table reserved for staff. A handful of others were seated in a

group, huddled together and talking in low voices. None of
them made room for Tessa to join them when she arrived
with her tray. Neither did they attempt to include her in the
conversation. She was not surprised.

Tessa pushed her food around the plate, wrapped up in
her thoughts. Every now and then she would surface from
her reverie, and each time she was slightly surprised to see
the meal before her. Finally she left the plate hardly
touched, and headed off for the staff room. At least there
she could pass the time with a newspaper if she was given
the cold shoulder.

Just before entering she became convinced that Greg
Roberts would already be in there, waiting for her,
desperate to start up the one-sided conversation that had
been so abruptly terminated that morning. The anxious
moment passed when Tessa saw that the sole occupant was
Mike Jenkins. He was dressed in a track suit and trainers
and had his feet up on the table. His eyes were closed and
the moment Tessa walked in he jumped in his seat,
swinging his trainers to the carpeted floor and casting a
guilty glance her way. "Oh," he said, slumping with relief.
"It's you."

"Lucky it wasn't The Dragon. You'd be in trouble."

Tessa got herself a coffee, retrieved one of the daily
papers from the pile on the windowsill and dropped into a
chair near him.

"Don't suppose you've heard anything?"

He did not have to explain what he meant.

Tessa shook her head. She almost mentioned her visit to
Chris Marshall's house last night, but thought better of it.
There was a chance word would get round and she could
find herself in an awkward situation, given that she had
taken the time to call there while the school head appeared
uninterested in doing so.

Still, it would be nice to have an ally.

"You know the police won't be interviewing us now?"

No, she didn't. What a surprise.

"They reckon there's no need. They're going to speak to
a couple of her closest friends but at home, not in school. It
sounds to me like they don't want to upset the other kids
unnecessarily. I'm surprised you hadn't been told."

"Nobody tells me anything." It was hard not to sound bitter.

He gave her a sympathetic look. "Don't let them bother you. They're a weird bunch. I must have been here two years before any of them gave me the time of day."

"Great. Only another eighteen months to go."

He grinned at that.

Tessa smiled back, raised the paper and pretended to read it. Her eyes skimmed over the words, not taking them in.

She looked up as the door opened. To her dismay it was Greg Roberts. He gave her his leering smile, but it vanished the moment he saw Mike Jenkins. Recovering quickly, he made a great show of peering around the staff room even though it was plain to see it was otherwise deserted.

"Either of you two seen Muriel?" he asked.

Tessa suspected that Roberts had really been looking for her, not The Dragon. "No. I haven't seen her all morning."

She had to force herself to talk to him.

"Me neither," Mike chipped in. "Tried her office?"

"Of *course* I've tried her office. First place I looked."

He gave them an ugly look and stalked out of the room, closing the door with a lot more force than was necessary. Tessa shuddered. It seemed he might have a temper, after all. Again she could not escape the feeling that she had good reason to be nervous around him. The more she saw, the less she liked.

"What a fucking jerk."

"Not in his fan club, Mike?"

"You could say that. And you?"

"He gives me the creeps."

The words were out before she could stop them. Thank God there had been no one else in the classroom.

Mike studied at her appraisingly. He gave the impression of someone wanting to say something they knew they shouldn't.

"You want to stay away from him," he said finally. "I mean it, Tessa. I've seen the way he looks at you."

"So have I. Like I said, he gives me the creeps."

"I can imagine. He's the wrong side of forty. He's never been married. Sounds a bit suspect to me."

A sudden gust of wind rattled the window. Although it was early afternoon the dull grey light made it seem closer to dusk. The playing fields floodlights were on, white flecks caught in their fierce beams like moths captivated by flame. Even in happier days Tessa had always considered January a dull month after the Christmas celebrations. Now it seemed to be not just dull but dead. Frozen days like this should be spent at home, behind closed curtains and in front of a fire. She could not wait for the weekend.

"If he gives you any grief, let me know."

His words warmed her. For the first time in God knew how long she felt as if there was someone who cared. Despite her earlier reluctance to confide in him she now felt a sudden urge to share her suspicions about Greg Roberts. She had wished for an ally and it appeared her wish had come true. A problem halved, as the saying went, was a problem shared.

Still, however, she found herself holding back.

It was not a question of whether she trusted him, more a case of what she was going to say.

That she thought Greg Roberts may have started an affair with a fourteen-year-old girl. That he may have murdered her, either in the heat of passion when she threatened to leave him or in cold blood when she threatened to expose their relationship. That she had nothing to support these allegations, other than a single sighting of Greg outside school and her instinctive dislike of the man. Tessa felt tightly coiled with frustration. She could not even be sure that anything bad had happened to Claire. The diary entries, as sinister and deeply upsetting as they had been, were not proof that the girl had been murdered. No, Tessa's conviction that she was dead was based solely on her dreams.

Unless Mike just happened to believe in supernatural phenomena she felt it best to keep her suspicions to herself.

"I will," she said. "And thanks."

The bell rang, startling her. She grimaced at the thought of having to return to the art room when she wanted to be home, with a glass of red wine and a good book. Her only consolation was that in just a few hours that was where she would be.

Mike yawned and stretched before pushing himself out of his chair with fluid ease. "Maybe I'll see you later."

He began to make his way to the door.

"Mike, wait."

What did she think she was doing?

"Is something wrong?"

"I was wondering if you fancied a drink this evening."

Inside she was mortified. At the same time she was glad she had spoken up. For the first time she felt like the wounds that Jonathan's betrayal had inflicted were, if not fully healed, then at least no longer raw and bleeding. Her sudden desire to ask Mike out was not born out of physical attraction. It was a recognition that she no longer wanted to spend her time alone. She was looking for human company, not sex. And, yes, if the opportunity to talk about her suspicions did at some point present itself she would seize it.

Mike looked surprised. To her relief he nodded. "Sure. You mean straight after work or do you want to meet up?"

Tessa always felt grubby at the end of the working day. It would be nice to have a shower before she went out for the night. "Would eight-thirty be okay? I'd like to get changed first."

"That's fine by me. Do you have somewhere in mind?"

Tessa hesitated. There was a pub in Bethesda, The Globe, but she did not fancy going anywhere too close to home. That was how gossip started. Neither did she want to return to Builth Wells, in case the threatened blizzard manifested. Then she remembered the Fox and Hounds, the pub on the road through Hebron. It was only a few miles from home but far enough away for her to feel comfortable with. She only knew one person living in the village and very much doubted Chris Marshall would be out that night.

"Do you know the Fox and Hounds in Hebron?"

"Sure. Nice pub."

"It's not too far out for you? I'm thinking about the weather."

"No. I've got a Land Rover. It's old but it can handle anything." He looked at his watch. "Anyway, I'd better get moving or the kids will be running riot in the gym. I'll see you tonight."

He smiled at her, and then left. Tessa knew that she really ought to be on her way to the art room by now, yet for some reason found she was reluctant to move. It was bad enough that she had risked embarrassing herself by asking Mike out. Now it was almost as if she was worried that by leaving the staff room immediately it would look like she was trying to follow him too.

Tessa found she was smiling. No wonder. She could not believe she had finally asked him, even if it had been purely on impulse. She closed her eyes and breathed in deeply, trying to clear her mind. It was no good. Tonight could be a triumph or it could as easily be a disaster. Mike could be looking on it as nothing more than a social interlude, two colleagues passing a few hours harmlessly. Then again, he could be thinking in terms of taking the first step towards a deeper relationship. After his initial surprise he had given nothing away. Tessa had no way of knowing which way he was taking it. Hell, she didn't know what *she* wanted.

It was too late to do anything about it now. She didn't mind if tonight wasn't quite a triumph. She just hoped it wasn't a disaster.

Standing outside the Fox and Hounds, an icy wind tugging at her hair and clothes, Tessa tried her best to compose herself, to at least attempt to project the appearance of calm even though she was churning inside. For a moment she felt like chickening out even if that would have made her feel twice as bad in the morning.

No. She was going through with this. If she could cope with a classroom full of rowdy kids she could handle a couple of drinks with a colleague. There was no budding romance; they were colleagues, possibly friends, nothing more.

The lounge was blissfully warm, but smoky enough to sting her eyes. There was no sign of Mike. Then again, Bethesda was only ten minutes away. Mike, who lived on the outskirts of Builth Wells, would have a much longer trip. She could forgive him being a little late, especially in this weather.

As she walked in she noticed a middle-aged man with grey hair reading a folded newspaper alone in a corner. He looked up at Tessa, nodded once, and then his eyes went back to the paper. At the bar a group of younger men sat on high stools, smoking, talking loudly. Bursts of laughter frequently punctured their conversation. From the look of them the pints on the counter before them were not their first. Tessa stood as far away along the bar from them as possible, waiting to be served.

"Where's Robbie tonight, then?" asked one of the group, a tall man who seemed pinned to the stool by his own excess fat.

One of his companions, a thin red-faced man, rolled his eyes theatrically. "He's away on a course. Some posh hotel."

"Another course," the big man snorted. "Fucking hell."

"Aye, well, you know Robbie. One promotion after another, he reckons. Bastard must be loaded."

A third voice piped up: "If you believe what *he* says, half the birds in the office want to shag him, he's so rich and important."

Loud laughter filled the air. Tessa looked impatiently behind the counter. She could see a lone barmaid, facing away from her, serving a couple of men in the other room. Tessa resisted the temptation to tap on the counter, knowing it would probably get the girl's back up. Then she heard the lounge door creak open and, glancing towards it, saw that Mike had finally arrived. He was wearing jeans and a thick black jacket. His race was ruddy from the cold.

He smiled apologetically as he reached her. "Sorry I'm late. I got stuck behind the slowest damned lorry in Mid Wales."

When the barmaid finally materialised Mike ordered a lager for himself and, after asking what she wanted, a dry white wine for Tessa. When their drinks arrived he carried them to a table at the farthest end of the room where it was slightly quieter and the air considerably less thick with cigarette smoke.

"So," he said when they were seated. "How's life in Bethesda?"

"Quiet. It's not exactly the big city."

"You're from London, aren't you?"

Tessa nodded.

"So what brought you here, the middle of nowhere?"

"I got divorced. Coming here was like making a clean break."

"Shit, I'm sorry." Mike's cheeks had actually reddened. "I wasn't trying to pry. I honestly had no idea you were married."

"Forget about it. It's yesterday's news. A couple of years ago I wouldn't have mentioned it. Now I think I've put it behind me."

Mike still looked embarrassed. He busied himself with his pint, looking aimlessly around the bar. Strangely, the more nervous he appeared, the more relaxed Tessa became. Now it seemed she was obliged to make him as comfortable as she felt.

"He was cheating on me," she said.

Mike put down his glass and looked at her. "You don't have to tell me about it, you know. I appreciate it's personal."

Tessa hesitated. Here they were, the first time they'd been out and, instead of ice-breaking chit-chat she had immediately dived into chapter one of the history of her divorce. Yet talking about it was liberating, almost exhilarating. It was like having an irritating splinter removed.

"To be honest, Mike, I've never told anyone about it before. After I made him admit it I sort of retreated into myself. Like it would all go away if I refused to accept it was happening."

"Was it anyone you knew?"

"Wendy? Not really. I met her at an office night out once, but only very briefly."

"How did you find out, if you don't mind me asking?"

Tessa's thoughts rewound. She had known about Jonathan's infidelity long before the night he confessed. The telephone calls when silence greeted her from the other end; Jonathan suddenly having to work on until nine or ten at night, supposedly because someone had left and he had to double up; and the faintest smell of perfume and cigarette smoke on his skin and clothes when he finally got home. Jonathan did not smoke. Neither, to the best of Tessa's knowledge, did he wear perfume.

"A friend of mine who worked in Jonathan's office told me about it. Everyone else knew what was going on. She couldn't bear the thought of me being the last to find out."

Mike shook his head slowly. "And you had no idea at all?"

"Oh no, I knew all right. I must have known about it for weeks if not months. I just wouldn't accept it was happening."

"I guess it must be hard to cover your tracks completely when you're having an affair."

"I hadn't thought of it in those terms," Tessa said, unable to resist a smile. "But you're right. All the telltale signs were there. Besides, even if they weren't I had – "

She broke off, suddenly realising that she had almost started talking about the dreams.

"You had what?"

"It's not important. Forget about it."

"Go on – what were you going to say?"

"All right, if you really want to know." The worst he could do, Tessa told herself, was think she was nuts. "I had a dream."

"What sort of dream?"

"I dreamed … I kept dreaming that Jonathan was making love to me, except it wasn't me. I can't really explain this but I saw and felt everything like it was happening for real, only to someone else." She couldn't bring herself to meet his eyes. "If you think that makes me seem crazy then I'd be the first to agree."

"I don't think you're crazy."

Well, thank God for that much at least. Tessa leant back in her chair and studied him. "You're full of surprises."

"Yeah, well, this might sound like a cliché but my Gran was from Dublin and I grew up with tales of the banshees and the little people, all the rest of it. When you've got Irish blood in you it's a lot easier to take that stuff seriously."

"Do you believe that what you dream about might have happened? Or that it might happen in the future?"

"Sure. We only use a small part of our brains, who knows what's going on in the rest of it?"

"I was convinced the dream was just my subconscious trying to wake me up to the facts. But like I said, it was so *real*. I felt like Jonathan was screwing me, except I was Wendy not Tessa."

"Is it the only dream like that you've had?"

"I've always been a dreamer since I was a kid. They were strange dreams, most of the time; weird images and faces that meant nothing to me. Now I think that maybe they did, except I had no way of knowing what. There *was* one time, though."

"Go on."

So Tessa told him the story of Molly Danvers, the old dear who had lived in the apartment above her and Jonathan's. Night after night Tessa dreamed of a large clock face, looming towards her. It held no obvious meaning or significance. Then one morning she had heard a loud crash from above. Racing upstairs and using the spare key Molly had left with her in case she ever locked herself out, Tessa had let herself into the old woman's apartment to find her lying semi-conscious on the floor, a fallen grandfather clock pinning her down. Tessa later found out that Molly had been trying to move it while she vacuumed, only for it to overbalance and fall onto her before she could move.

"The point is, I'd been in her apartment dozens of times and still didn't put two and two together. Molly had some nasty cuts and bruises. But it could have been a lot worse. What if she'd died? I would have had to have lived with the knowledge that I could have saved her, if only I'd figured out what the dream meant."

"Not necessarily," Mike said. He had, Tessa noticed, barely touched his drink. Come to that, she realised she had barely touched hers. "Maybe you were never meant to prevent the accident from happening, only to help her afterwards. It's like the old saying goes; some things are meant to happen."

Tessa instinctively knew that the time was right. She hadn't been planning to raise it but neither had she expected Mike to have been so responsive.

"There's something else," she said.

"Another strange dream?"

"Yes. About Claire."

He reacted as if she'd slapped him. "Jesus."

"I know why the police don't think it's necessary to come into the school any more. Claire had a boyfriend. He was a lot older than her. They may have run off together."

"You know all this from a *dream*?"

"No." Tessa made herself silently count to three before continuing. She needed to gather her thoughts. By rushing into the story, not telling it in the correct order, all she would do was confuse him and maybe lose his sympathy too.

"I went to see Claire's mother last night. I thought it was the right thing to do. She took me up to Claire's room to show me some pictures. The kid's a really talented artist. Anyway, she had to run off and answer the phone and, well, I found Claire's diary. She'd hidden it."

"And presumably that's how you found out about the older boyfriend." Mike looked and sounded genuinely shocked.

"Yes. I gave it to Chris – Mrs Marshall – and when I left she was going to call the police. Claire doesn't have a big circle of friends. Her mother has probably named the few she did have and they will probably talk to them about it. But I don't think they'll be of much help. I think she was keeping it a secret from them too."

She could have said a lot more, but at that stage it seemed wiser to give Mike time to take in what she'd told him.

He sipped at his lager. "If she has run off with this boyfriend, isn't that good news? Better than if she'd just vanished into thin air?"

"I wish it was. But from what I read, the boyfriend is quite a nasty piece of work. He made it pretty clear what he'd do to her if she told anyone about them, or if she tried to finish it."

"Christ, I see what you mean. That doesn't sound good."

"There's more. I said I'd been dreaming about Claire. A really awful dream, like I'm burning and then I'm drowning in freezing water. The worst thing was I couldn't move. It felt like someone was pushing me under, holding me down."

"Did this dream start before or after you found the diary?"

"I know what you're thinking. That what I read might have shaped the dream. I wish I could say that was true, but the fact is that I'd been having the dream *before* I found it."

"It doesn't mean anything, not for certain. For all you know you could be dreaming about someone else, someone you've never met and never will meet, not about Claire at all."

"That is possible but I *know* it's about Claire. Don't ask me how I know. I just do."

He stared at her. Tessa could not read his expression, did not know whether he was angry, sad or just confused.

"Is that it? Or do you have any more surprises in store?"

"Maybe we'd better leave it there."

"If there's more, you might as well tell me."

"It's just a feeling, a suspicion. I can't prove it's true."

"Tell me. Then I'll tell *you* whether I believe you."

She felt as if she were picking her way through a minefield. It was one thing telling Mike about her dreams; even if he did not believe her, there was no real harm. But once she started pointing the finger she would be playing for much higher stakes. The question was did she trust Mike enough to confide in him?

"Tessa," he said softly. "Please, tell me. I might be able to help. Even if I can't, wouldn't you feel better for talking about it?"

She was not sure that she would. What she *was* certain of was that keeping her suspicions to herself would not help Claire. If Tessa had to share them with anyone, it might as well be Mike.

"Go on," he prompted.

"Okay." Unable to find a way of softening the blow, Tessa decided to come right out and speak her mind. "I can't prove anything but I think Greg Roberts could be involved."

Mike stared at her. Then he gave a low whistle. He leant forward in his chair, as if afraid of being overheard. "That is one hell of an accusation to make, Tessa, especially with no proof."

"I know! It's just a suspicion based on things I've seen. I could never go to the police with it. They would probably arrest me for wasting their time, and to be honest I wouldn't blame them."

"What makes you think Greg has anything to do with this?"

"Claire wrote in her diary that if their relationship was ever discovered, he would lose his job."

"You could say the same about any teacher, me included."

"I haven't finished yet. The other morning I got ambushed by him walking into school. A few girls passed us, about the same age as Claire. The look he gave them, Mike. If you ask me, he's the type of weirdo who gets turned on by schoolgirls."

"All right, you may have a point. He's always struck me as a bit weird, a bit of a peeping tom. But it's a big step from imagining him getting turned on by kids to picturing him … you know."

"You should have seen the expression on his face. Maybe then you'd think twice about that. Oh, and there's something else. The night I went to see Claire's mother, I saw Greg driving past, very slowly, staring at the street where she lives."

"Maybe he was just curious, what with Claire disappearing."

"Do you know Claire's address?"

"Me? No. Why should I?"

"If you don't know, how come Greg does?"

"You found out, didn't you?"

"That was different, Mike. I looked up her details so I could visit her mother, see if there was any way I could help. Greg wasn't there to pay a social call. But he *was* having a very close look."

Something else occurred to her. "In the dream I was being held down under the water. I couldn't break free, no matter how hard I struggled. That would take a lot of strength. I know Greg's gone to seed a bit, but he's still a big bear of a man."

Mike pursed his lips and shook his head. Then he picked up his empty glass. "I need another drink. Want one?"

"Let me get these," Tessa said, reaching for her purse, but Mike insisted and she didn't feel like arguing the point. She waited impatiently for him to return from the bar. The moment he put their fresh drinks on the table she said: "I've told you all this because I trust you."

"And I'm glad that you trust me. Even so, it doesn't change the fact that neither of us can do anything about it. If Greg is behind this – and it's a very big *if* – then unless he has a sudden crisis of conscience and confesses, we could never prove it."

Tessa nodded and sighed. That was the worst of it.

She heard the muted trill of a mobile phone and realised it was hers, zipped away inside her fleece pocket.

"Excuse me a moment," she said. She took the mobile out and glanced briefly at the display. It was a local code but she did not recognise the number. "Hello?"

"Is that Tessa?"

"Yes."

"Tessa, this is Chris Marshall."

Her voice sounded tight with emotion.

Tessa's mouth went dry. Her stomach rolled. "Have you heard from her?" she asked, anticipating the answer but needing to ask the question anyway, for the sake of having something to say.

"No. But you asked me to tell you if there was any news. The police are going to start searching the woods tomorrow."

Burning heat, and then freezing cold. Hands pressed down on her shoulders, holding her under. She tried to hold her breath but her lungs were bursting and she instinctively opened her mouth, letting in a flood of icy cold water. Above her the light was strong, the silhouette of her killer distorted by water. It grew bigger, as though he were bending over her, perhaps anxious to witness the moment that life her slipped away. Then, in the final seconds before darkness engulfed her, it was as if the water had parted and she caught a fleeting glimpse of flesh ...

Tessa stood at the art room window, staring out into the slate grey morning and wondering if the police had found anything yet. She felt guilty for not being with Chris Marshall, aware of how irrational that was but still not able to shake off the feeling. Tessa had a responsibility to the children, while Claire's mother would have plenty of family and friends to console her now that events had taken such a dramatic new turn. The police had brought in tracker dogs, while volunteers from Hebron and Bethesda were lining up to join the search. It had been on the Welsh TV news that morning. Watching it, Tessa had been close to tears.

She had hoped to bump into Mike before classes started but, as luck would have it, there was no sign of him. Tessa owed him an apology. Last night's call had left her feeling lower than she could remember since the break-up with Jonathan. The pub walls had seemed to close in on her. All she had wanted to do was get out of there. Mike had been more understanding than Tessa had any right to expect. After all, she was the one who had asked him out, and there she was, crying off early. But he had insisted it was all right. In fact he had looked pretty shaken when Tessa told him who had called, and why. He had walked her to her car, wished her a safe journey home, then waited until she was on her way out of the pub car park.

What made it all the more frustrating was that she believed they had really connected; that Mike, while hardly convinced that she was right about Greg Roberts, had at least been willing to hear her out without laughing in her face or, worse, telling someone else of her fanciful and groundless suspicions. Neither had he tried to convince her that she was wrong, to forget the whole stupid idea. He had gone up several notches in her estimation for that.

Aware there was nothing else she could do, Tessa vowed to keep a very close eye on Greg Roberts. He might slip, might do or say something that she could seize on and use against him. Tessa had no idea what that might be, but she would be waiting with eyes and ears open.

Unfortunately, that would mean having to stay fairly close to him, during school time at least. Tessa would never take up his offer of a game of badminton or anything else he might suggest. While she was in St David's Tessa felt safe. Outside the school grounds, without the company of others, she would be vulnerable. There was no point in exposing herself to danger, not when the chances of gaining anything from it were so slim.

The morning seemed to take an age to pass. By the time the bell rang to signal lunch, Tessa felt so sick with anxiety that she could not stomach the thought of eating. She glanced out the window; the light was poor and a fierce wind punished the stands of trees that surrounded the school. There was snow in the air; not the kind of weather for a stroll into town.

Spurning the dining hall, Tessa instead made her way to the staff room, hoping to find Mike. As she walked in she saw him, stood talking to Kathleen Brennan, an English teacher who had perhaps exchanged two or three sentences with Tessa in all the months that she had been at the school.

"You seem very friendly with the Ice Maiden," she was saying loudly, her back to Tessa. "Tell me, does she have any feelings or is there a big block of ice where her heart should be?"

Tessa thought, *The Ice Maiden? Who are they talking about?*

She knew the answer straight away.

Mike looked over Kathleen's shoulder towards the door, realised that Tessa had just walked in and said hastily, "Excuse me a moment, Helen. I need to have a word with Tessa."

He smiled uncertainly as he approached, taking Tessa gently by the arm and leading her to one side. "I was going to look for you in the art room if you didn't show. Everything all right?"

Tessa nodded, too angry and upset to speak. The Ice Maiden; how long had they been calling her that?

"If they are still searching the woods at the weekend I'm going to volunteer. Want to join me?"

Tessa knew he was making an effort for her sake, but his attempt at friendliness fell flat. "Maybe," she said, moving away.

"Wait," he said. "I guess you overheard what she was saying. Don't let it get to you. You know what they're like."

Tessa caught sight of Brennan looking with too-casual disinterest her way, and kept her voice deliberately low. "The Ice Maiden, for Christ's sake? That's rich. They ignore me since I arrive and then try to make out that *I'm* the cold one."

Mike looked as if he wanted to ground to open up and swallow him. Tessa relented. She doubted he was involved in the little cabal that appeared to have been formed against her. She had a stubborn streak that she normally fought to control. Now she gave it free reign. Tessa had worked with the petty and downright nasty before; this lot were amateurs compared to some of the bitches she'd known.

"Forget it," she said. "They're not worth worrying about. Oh, and yes, I'll definitely join you at the search. To be honest I can't help but think I should be there now, volunteering, not here."

"Have you spoken to Chris since last night?"

"No. I didn't like to call." Tessa could imagine Chris starting at the sound of the telephone, her heart breaking anew each time she answered only to find it was not her daughter on the line.

With a feeling of satisfaction she saw Kathleen Brennan turn and amble away from them, clearly trying to create the impression that she was bored. Tessa was glad she had kept her temper in check. That would have given the cabal something else to talk about. "I might call tonight if she hasn't been in touch by then."

"Let me know what she says. You've got my number."

He had given it to her last night. Just in case, he'd said.

"The moment I hear anything, I'll let you know."

Tessa still did not feel hungry, so she bought coffee for the two of them and they sat in a corner, away from the others, passing the time in idle chatter. Every now and then the window would rattle. Snow and icy rain scratched at the glass. The storm that had been threatening all week did not seem too far off.

The bell rang. As she walked along the corridor, kids flowing round her like a river round a rock, Tessa saw

Greg Roberts heading in the opposite direction. Was it her imagination, or did his eyes follow a couple of older girls, their large breasts trying to break free of their blouses? His beefy face gleamed with sweat and his hands were pushed deep into his trouser pockets. As she passed the school office Tessa was tempted to turn and duck into the open doorway on some pretext or other, only resisting by telling herself she would learn nothing about Greg Roberts if she kept avoiding him. As he approached she steeled herself for the inevitable conversation, the fresh attempt to persuade her to play that game of badminton.

Greg, however, did not stop.

He did not even offer his usual leering smile.

The look he *did* give her was witheringly blank.

Tessa quickly looked away, caught completely wrong-footed. Either Greg was in one hell of a bad mood about something, or …

No, she told herself. It wasn't possible. There was no way Greg could possibly know about her suspicions. Not unless Mike had told him, or told anyone else in the school; the story would have spread like wildfire. Certainly she could not dismiss that possibility out of hand but every instinct told her Mike would never have done that. His own remarks about the man had been less than complimentary. Greg was in a bad mood, that was all.

Still, she was unnerved. It felt like the rules had changed. Before, she had known where she stood with Greg; suffer his persistence with a brave smile and keep him at arm's length without him catching on. If for some reason he had not just lost interest but was pointedly snubbing her she wanted to know why.

One other possibility suggested itself; that Greg had found out about her and Mike meeting up last night.

That, God help her, he was jealous.

Tessa felt icy fingers run down her spine. If Greg *was* the obsessive type, if he *was* capable of killing his schoolgirl lover, how would he react to Tessa seeing another man? There was no romance between her and Mike, not even the slightest hint of it. But at the same time Greg would have no way of knowing that.

By the time she reached the art room Tessa began to feel that she was in this way over her head.

She had to admit it; she was afraid.

If Claire was dead and if Greg had killed her, what worried Tessa was the prospect of him, alone again, deciding to cast his net around for a replacement lover.

What was he capable of doing if he was spurned? Or, worse yet, if in his twisted mind he believed he had been betrayed?

Tessa paused outside the art room, not yet ready for the chaos that awaited her. She took a few deep breaths. Okay, maybe she was being melodramatic. There were all kinds of reasons to explain why he had appeared so pissed off. Some classes were good and some were bad; maybe Greg just had an afternoon of rotten lessons ahead of him. His car could have had a flat tyre. His cat may have died.

There was no point jumping to conclusions.

The ceaseless energy of the kids helped push her worries to the back of her mind and the afternoon passed quickly. When the bell rang for the last time that day, Tessa did not drag her feet. The moment the kids were gone she was out of the door, locking in the mess and dirty brushes they had left in their wake. That could all wait until the morning. For now, she just wanted to get out of the place as fast as she could, before she could bump into Greg Roberts or Kathleen Brennan or any member of her bitchy secret society. The Ice Maiden indeed. If Tessa was so cold-hearted, how come she was the only one who had taken the time to call on Claire's mother?

The wind hit her like a slap when she walked out of the side door. Tessa groaned and pulled up her fleece collar but that did nothing to protect her face, which felt like it was being flayed. The sky was the colour of something long dead. Fat flakes of snow tumbled from it and a veneer of white coated the path to the car park. Tessa had no choice but to walk slowly; even the rubber soles of her boots were struggling to find a grip.

A layer of snow maybe half an inch deep had accumulated on the Escort's rear windscreen. Tessa swiped at it with her gloves until she had cleared the worst of it away. By chance she glanced back at the school building.

The lights inside blazed. Her eyes were drawn to Greg's room and she could see he was standing at the window, looking out. Logic dictated that the darkness outside and the bright light inside meant he could see nothing but reflections. Even so, Tessa could not shake off the feeling that Greg was staring at her. Then a gust of wind, strong enough to rock the Escort and so cold that her eyes immediately filled with tears, made her quickly turn away and busy herself with unlocking the door.

Driving out of the car park, wheels sounding like they were going over hundreds of tiny shells, Tessa glanced in the rear view mirror and noticed Mike's Land Rover.

She was sorry she had missed him. While she was still livid about the Ice Maiden tag, her anger was directed solely at the others and she wanted him to know that. Never mind, she thought. He had given her his number and she could always call him later.

Snow started to fall in earnest and the wipers struggled to keep the windscreen clear. Headlights from oncoming vehicles blinded her and Tessa was glad when she finally left the main road and began to follow the winding route to Bethesda. The surface was still only lightly dusted and the temperature had not fallen sufficiently to crust the snow with ice. If that happened overnight then she would not be going to school the next morning; the road would be lethal.

By the time she reached the cottage, Tessa's shoulders were stiff with tension and a dull ache had developed behind her eyes. Her light-headedness was probably down to the fact that she had not eaten since breakfast. While hunger still eluded her, she knew she had to force something down. Not feeling up to spending much time in the kitchen she rustled up a cheese and ham omelette and picked at it without tasting much.

Just after six the phone rang. It was Jan, the school secretary. Word had come down from the county council. A big snowfall was expected in the next day or so. The schools were being closed until after the weekend, rather than to chance having the kids arrive in the morning only to have to send them back home.

Putting the phone down, Tessa could not decide whether this was good news or bad. Being away from such an oppressive, unfriendly atmosphere was hardly a burden. Then again, it meant three days of isolation, especially if the storm was as bad as forecast and she found herself trapped in the cottage. Provisions were not a problem, as she regularly topped up her stocks of fresh milk and kept a tin of dried in the pantry, just in case. There was plenty of bread in the freezer, along with packs of vegetables and meat, and dozens of tins in the cupboards.

She may find herself bored to death, but at least she would not go hungry.

Tessa dozed, only to be jerked awake by a strident ringing. She rubbed her eyes and peered blearily at the wall clock, surprised to find that it was almost nine.

She reached out for the phone, but as her hands closed round the receiver, the ringing stopped. Within seconds it started again, making her jump. She did not answer it immediately. Whoever was calling could not count patience as one of their virtues. The first name to spring to mind was Greg Roberts.

"Hello?" Tessa never gave out her number.

"Tessa, it's Mike."

"Oh hi, Mike. Listen, I'm sorry I missed you before I left. I was going to give you a call but I fell asleep."

"That's okay. I was just ringing to make sure you'd heard."

"About the school being closed? Yes, they rang."

"Not about the school. I meant about the search."

She was almost afraid to ask. "What about it?"

"It was on the Welsh news earlier."

Tessa almost swore. She would have seen it for herself if she had not drifted off.

"They said the police were sending divers into the lake first thing in the morning. They're worried about this blizzard that's supposed to blowing in,"

Tessa's hand hurt. She realised she was squeezing the receiver so tight that her knuckles had turned white. She forced herself to relax and tried to rein in the thoughts that were running out of control in her head. "Will they have enough time?"

"They think so. The really heavy snow isn't expected until late afternoon, and it's not a really big lake."

Tessa fell silent. What Mike had said was right. It was at most a half-hour walk around the lake. But it was deep in parts and there were all kinds of hidden dangers lurking under its surface. She did not envy the divers, especially as she could not rid herself of the feeling that she already knew what they would find.

"Tessa, are you okay?"

"I will be. It's just that, well, this is happening so quickly."

Wasn't that true. Monday was just two days ago. Tessa could not believe what had happened since then.

She doubted Chris Marshall could believe it, either.

Not wanting to be drawn into a conversation about it, she thanked Mike for ringing and said she'd call tomorrow. He sounded slightly disappointed at her haste to get off the line.

Tessa stared at the phone, wondering if she should pick it up and call Chris. It was impossible to imagine what the woman was going through. Having your only child fail to return home was dreadful in itself. But there was always hope, the belief that at any moment they were going to walk in through the door, having realised that, for whatever reason they had left in the first place, they didn't like being out there in the world, all alone.

But surely by now Chris, just like Tessa, would have sensed that this story would have no such happy ending.

On impulse Tessa reached for the phone, only to waver.

She could not bring herself to do it, could not bear to hear the disappointment in Chris's voice when she answered.

Tessa slumped back in the chair and rubbed her eyes, feeling tiredness and depression start to drag her down. Outside the wind moaned in sympathy with her mood. Snow brushed the window with feathery fingers. It was not a night to be outdoors. Neither, Tessa thought sadly, was it a night to be indoors, alone.

For a moment she wanted to call Mike back, to invite him round, even offer him the spare room if the weather turned bad.

What made her resist was an awareness of what that might lead to. She was not quite ready to be led into temptation.

Not yet, she thought; maybe one day soon, but not yet.

Burning heat, and then freezing cold. She fought against the hands that held her down. There was ice in her lungs. Blackness filled her vision. The dark outline of her killer swirled above her. And then, as if her mind had freed itself from her body, she felt herself rise through the water and a face began to swim into focus...

The lake was roughly circular, its waters slate grey and turbulent, mirroring the brooding sky above. Overnight the temperature had plunged. Not long after dawn Tessa had jerked out of sleep, still trembling from the dream's power, to find that the world outside had turned white. At least a foot of snow obscured everything. This was not a day for venturing far outdoors, but even before she had turned in last night she knew where she would be going; the lake.

Its siren song called to her, too strong to resist.

Now, having struggled up the snowy path through the trees, taking twice as long as usual, she wondered if she had done the right thing. On the far side of the choppy water she could see Chris Marshall deep in conversation with a police officer, presumably one of high rank. Others clustered round them in a loose circle, as if trying to protect them from the frigid wind that was doing its best to rip the surrounding trees from the ground. A handful of police Range Rovers and a large white van – which Tessa guessed had been used to carry the diving gear up the single track from Bethesda – were parked nearby. A team of maybe six divers were taking it in turns to go into the water in pairs. Tessa had seen one changeover in the short time she had been there; the two emerging from the lake immediately rushing into the white van which no doubt would have heaters waiting; the lake must be almost unbearably cold.

A hundred or so yards to Tessa's left was a tree-flanked opening. It marked the end of the footpath from Hebron, a fair hike away. According to the late news bulletin, which

Tessa had made herself stay awake for, the police search in the forest had revealed no indication that Claire and her boyfriend – *killer* – had passed through. That proved nothing. Footprints would have been obscured and poor light would have hampered the rescuers further. Had they been in the wood, the lake was their most likely destination; hence the divers.

But even if they found the body, they still might not find the killer. If Claire had been in the water for the best part of five days, then all the forensics and DNA technology in the world might not be enough. Perhaps the killer had known that. He might well have done if he was an intelligent man; a science teacher, perhaps.

Tessa knew that all she had to do was pick up the phone and make an anonymous call, giving Greg's name. The police could take it from there; she would have done all she could.

Twice the dream had come frustratingly close to revealing who had held Claire down in the doomed girl's final few seconds. If Tessa had actually seen Greg's face, then she would have called the police.

If at any time she did she his face, she decided, she would call the police. Until then she would leave well enough alone.

The wind, laden with ice, stung her face and blurred her vision so she began to stroll counter-clockwise around the lake, towards the cluster of police vehicles. Even if she eventually could not bring herself to approach Chris, she would be close to the track. It emerged near the park at the opposite end of Bethesda from Tessa's cottage but, with hindsight, she knew it would be a quicker and easier route home than slipping and sliding back down the forest path. As she walked her gaze alternated between Chris Marshall and the divers in the water. At any moment she expected one of them to shout out or start waving, an indication that something had been found. But so far there had been nothing.

Around her the trees swished and creaked alarmingly, sounding as if they were close to falling over. The snow had stopped but the odd fat flake still swirled through the air, catching in Tessa's eyelashes and making her blink.

Instead of brightening as the hours passed, the sky was growing slowly but noticeably darker.

Would they find Claire's body before the weather forced them to give up?

It would be a close call. Part of Tessa wanted one of the divers to give that dreaded signal. At least then Chris would know the true fate of her daughter, as heartbreaking as that might be. Another part desperately hoped that the search would remain fruitless. Tessa was certain she would not be able to cope with watching Claire's body being pulled from the water, nor with the sight of Chris reacting to it. And yet she knew in her heart that the moment would only be delayed and that Claire was somewhere beneath those stormy waters, waiting to be found.

When she got to the track she was surprised to find Mike standing a yard or two away from her, out of sight of the police and Chris Marshall. He lifted a hand in greeting and smiled with little enthusiasm. Tessa hurried over to him. Once the surprise of seeing him there had worn off she was glad to have someone else to talk to. "I didn't think I'd see you here today," she said.

Mike shrugged. He wore walking boots, waterproof leggings and a matching jacket. A woollen cap was pulled over his ears and his hands were protected from the brutal elements by thick gloves. In Tessa's eyes he looked the real outdoors type. But then, she supposed, given that he was a sports teacher that was no surprise.

"I tried to call you earlier," he said. "I was worried."

"I've been up here, watching."

"Have you spoken to Claire's mother yet?"

Tessa shook her head. "I've been trying to summon the courage. But between what she must be going through right now and with so many police around I just couldn't make myself do it."

"At least there are no TV people here. She must be feeling bad enough as it is, without a camera stuck in her face."

"Probably the weather put them off."

The conversation petered out, both of them distracted by the lakeside. Chris had disappeared; she was probably sitting in one of the police cars, trying to keep warm and no doubt trying to keep herself together at the same time. God, she must be going through absolute hell.

A particularly savage gust of frigid wind struck Tessa full in the face, making her gasp. She could not stick these conditions much longer, as well wrapped as she was. Standing still was not helping; although her boots were insulated her toes were going numb. Slowly, wincing as the feeling returned, she walked to the edge of the lake and looked down into the water. A vision of Claire, blonde hair drifting sluggishly in the depths, sprang to mind and Tessa shook her head in an effort to dislodge the image. Wherever the girl was now, she could never be hurt again. That may be scant consolation but it was the best she could come up with.

The water was clear and Tessa saw that the bed was covered in stones. Once Claire had stopped struggling, had her killer filled her pockets with them and pulled her away from the shoreline? The edge of the lake was shallow but Tessa had been told that it sloped sharply away. He would only have had to have dragged the lifeless body out so far, then gravity would have taken care of the rest.

Tessa shuddered as a cold that had nothing to do with the weather ran through her.

She went back to Mike, boots scrunching in the snow. He was staring at the ground and looked up as she approached, face pale and serious. Tessa remembered that he had known Claire far longer than she had. "Any more standing around in this weather and I'll be the Ice Maiden for real."

It was a fairly weak attempt at levity which only served to make him look uncomfortable. "Yeah, well, like I told you, don't listen to them. They haven't got anything better to do."

Tessa still could not believe they thought she was the standoffish one. "Is that how you see me – all cold and aloof?"

He shook his head quickly. "Of course I don't."

"But the others do, that much is obvious."

"To tell you the truth I think they're a little afraid of you."

It was such an unexpected response that Tessa laughed. "Why in God's name would they be afraid of me?"

"Oh, you know, an art teacher coming down from a big school in London to little old St David's. To them it probably felt like having Steven Spielberg turn up to teach media studies."

"It was bigger than St David's, I admit, but not *that* big. And while I like to think I'm a good teacher I'm certainly no Spielberg."

"But you've had your own art exhibitions."

Tessa almost laughed again. "Where'd you hear that?"

"They seem to think you have."

"If they'd bothered to ask I'd have put them straight."

"I expect they were waiting for you to make the first move."

"Hey, don't forget I was the stranger in town. They all knew each other. I didn't know anyone. I was a bag of nerves."

Mike nodded. "I believe you. But, like I said, they were under the impression you were this hotshot teacher. Because you didn't go round chatting to everyone I think they took it the wrong way."

There was nothing Tessa could say to that. How easy it was for the truth to become distorted, twisted out of shape into a huge misconception. She had blamed them, they had blamed her and all along neither had been at fault. Maybe it was not too late to put it right; only time would tell. But now that Tessa knew where the others were coming from she could at least try to deal with it.

It occurred to her that her suspicions about Greg Roberts might be just as much of a misconception. The more she thought about it, the more it struck her that she really had nothing to base it on other than an instinctive dislike of the man. Okay, so there was no denying he was a bit of a letch, but he was certainly not alone. And why shouldn't he have been in Hebron that evening? For all Tessa knew he was out visiting. Once the idea of his guilt had popped into her mind she had embraced it all too willingly. Now she wondered if that was because the only way she could deal with Claire's death was by finding someone to blame.

Snow began to fall heavily. Movement by the police cars caught Tessa's eye. Chris Marshall was out in the open again, only this time she was not alone. A tall man was stood with her, one arm around her shoulder. It could be her ex, her boyfriend or a brother. Tessa knew virtually nothing about the woman. But the sight of him so close to Chris made Tessa feel that to approach them now would be to intrude on a moment that was meant to be private.

Two divers clambered out of the water, none replaced them. Chris and her companion must have emerged from the shelter of the police car in order to witness the suspension of the underwater search. Doubtless it would not be safe to continue with the weather taking a turn for the worse. It was with a heavy heart that Tessa turned away from the lake. Claire's fate would have to remain undetermined until after the blizzard had blown itself out and possibly much longer than that.

There was always the chance that her body would never be found, that Chris Marshall would spend the rest of her life wondering. Tessa could not dwell on that. It was too depressing.

"Looks like that's it," she said as she approached Mike.

"I guessed that as soon as I saw the snow come down."

Without saying anything further they began to make their way down the track. Tessa wanted to be off the hillside before the fleet of police vehicles passed. Watching the search under way had felt voyeuristic, almost ghoulish, and she did not want Chris to know she had been there. At least the rutting caused by the passing of so many tyres made the going a little easier. Snow filled the air around them but she was able to follow the track easily enough, even with visibility restricted by the shifting white clouds.

It was unnaturally quiet and Tessa realised the wind had dropped to little more than a whisper. The trees had ceased their restless creaking. All she could hear was her and Mike's laboured breathing and the crunch of their boots in the snow. It felt like the world was holding its breath, waiting for something to happen.

The track was only just about wide enough to accommodate the largest of the police vans, and the forestry came right up to the edge on both sides. Tessa caught herself glancing nervously into the woods. But beyond the falling snow she could see nothing but shadows where anyone or anything could be watching and waiting.

She was glad Mike was with her.

"Have you had any more dreams?"

His voice, sounding so loud, startled her. "Uh-huh."

"No more details, nothing that would help?"

"I wish there was, Mike, I really do. The worst thing is, I feel like I'm so close to seeing whoever it was that held her down."

"And what would you do if you *do* get to see him?"

Tessa thought about that. "I've been asking myself the same question. And the honest answer is, I don't know."

It was the best part of twenty minutes before they emerged from the forest. They had barely exchanged another word all the way down; it had taken all of their energy and concentration to avoid slipping. Once clear of the trees the track cut through a grassy area, eventually terminating at the park. They walked through it, passing children running riot, screaming with laughter as they pelted each other with snowballs.

Despite the inconvenience that the weather caused, Tessa loved it. Bethesda was a pleasant village but when it wore its winter coat it was magnificent. It brought back magical memories of her childhood in Hampshire, of Christmases spent in the big old house with its beamed ceilings and log fires.

They had been happy, innocent times.

Long lost now, she thought with a tinge of sadness.

Mike had left the Land Rover outside the small cluster of shops opposite the park. He must have been really concerned about her to have made such a long journey in such conditions, four wheel drive or not. His thoughtfulness touched her. She knew very few people, if any, who would have shown the same consideration.

"Whereabouts do you live?" he asked, as they crossed the deserted road.

"Not far from here."

He reached into his coat pocket and pulled out a bunch of keys. "Jump in. I'll give you a lift back."

"There's no need. Honestly, I can walk it."

"I think we've both done enough walking for one day. Come on, jump in – it's not like I'll be going miles out of my way."

Tessa directed him along Church Road until they reached the lane that branched off it. "This is fine," she said.

"Are you sure?"

"See that cottage up there? That's mine. I can be there in a minute or two and it'll save you having to reverse."

"Nice place."

"One of the benefits of divorcing a rich bastard," Tessa said as she opened the door. She paused. Mike had made a real effort. The least she could do was invite him in. "I was going to make lunch. You're welcome to join me if you're not in any rush."

He peered out at the falling snow. For a second Tessa thought he was going to say yes, but then he frowned. "Better not. This old monster can cope with most conditions but I think it's getting worse. Thanks anyway – maybe we can do it another time."

"That would be nice."

She stepped down, boots sinking deep into the snow, and slammed the door shut. She heard Mike ram the Land Rover into gear and then it was moving off. The horn sounded twice, echoing around the empty street, and Tessa lifted one arm in response before turning and starting to pick her way along the lane. She was disappointed that Mike had declined her offer. It would have been nice to have had some company, but now it seemed a long, empty day awaited her. There was only so much daytime TV she could stomach and she was not in the mood for reading.

She hoped to God the snow would stop soon, or else her home would start to feel more like a prison.

She was burning. Her lungs were clogged with smoke. She tried to scream but no words came out. And then there was no heat, only cold; a fierce, bone-penetrating chill so intense that it burned as much as the fire. Again she tried to call out but liquid ice poured down her throat. A rushing sound filled her ears and she knew she was under water. She began to struggle as her body cried out for air, but she could not move. There was a weight on her shoulders which she fought against. Yet no matter how violently she thrashed about she could not free herself from the force that held her under. Her struggles weakened as she exhaled the last of the air in her lungs. Suddenly the pressure on her shoulders relaxed but even then she could not move. Above her the light was strong. It framed a shadow which loomed closer until she could make out the distorted outline of a human figure; her killer. It grew bigger, as though he were bending over her, perhaps anxious to witness the moment that life her slipped away. In the final seconds before darkness engulfed her, it was as if her soul had let go of her body and she felt herself rise. Then the waters parted and she saw Mike Jenkins looking down at her, eyes wide, face contorted ...

Tessa gasped as she woke. For a moment she was utterly disorientated, convinced she was still in the water, dying. Even when she realised she was in bed, she still could not believe that she was alive and safe. Her body began to spasm with cold and fear. She grabbed the quilt and pulled it round her, holding it tight for comfort as much as for warmth. Daylight filled the room but her mind was still trapped in the darkness of the dream.

Mike Jenkins, not Greg Roberts, had murdered Claire.

No, Tessa thought wildly, it couldn't be.

"Oh God," she groaned.

She wanted to believe that she had seen Mike's face only because he had been in her thoughts for the last few days. It was only natural she would dream of him.

But she knew that was not true.

The dream had always felt real. That was what had made it so powerful. Tessa had never doubted that it had shown her Claire's final moments of life. Had the face been revealed as that of Greg Roberts then she would have accepted his guilt without doubt. Why then, when Mike's was the face revealed to her, was she trying to persuade herself that she was wrong?

The truth was that she did not like Greg Roberts but she did like Mike. She could understand how Claire may have had a crush on him. All the qualities that she found attractive in him – his good looks, his self-effacing nature and his eagerness to help – would be just as alluring to a teenage girl. Possibly more so as Claire would not have possessed the years of life experience that had made Tessa hold back.

It was impossible to believe that he was a killer.

Tessa had socialised with him. Hell, she had invited him into her home.

It struck her then that he really *had* gone out of his way to travel to Bethesda yesterday. He may have had a Land Rover but it was still a risky journey across the mountain roads with the snow almost knee-deep in places. Was it possible that he had not been motivated by concern for Tessa? For all she knew he was there out of a warped sense of guilt, or even perhaps to keep a closer eye on developments, ready to bolt if Claire's body was found.

She pushed herself up on the bed.

Something about their conversation yesterday nagged at her, but she just could not remember what.

The clock caught her eye. It was gone nine. Exhausted from yesterday's exertions she had slept ten hours straight.

She went to the window and pulled back the curtains, squinting at the sudden sharp light. Snow lay thickly on the ground, obscuring everything. Tessa shivered and let the curtain fall back into place. The world looked too cold and lifeless.

She headed for the shower. Normally she wouldn't bother closing the bathroom door. Now she did not like the thought of leaving it open. So she showered with the door locked, staying under the water as briefly as possible, convinced that when she opened the door again, she would not be alone.

She dressed and went downstairs, straight to the kitchen where she put the kettle on, craving coffee. Her nerves were stretched taut and she caught herself gnawing on her fingernails. Unable to stand still she moved into the living room, switching on the lamps rather than opening the curtains. She flicked on the TV, volume low, for company rather than because she had any intention of watching.

Maybe her compulsion to keep moving was nothing more than a smokescreen, a way of avoiding the question that she had been trying not to ask since she woke.

Now that she had seen his face in her dream, what was she going to do? Yesterday she had decided that, if she did see the killer, she would call the police, make an anonymous call which she thought would be enough to prove to herself that she had done all she could but without getting directly involved.

The trouble was she had made that decision when she was almost certain that she would see Greg Roberts.

Now it did not seem quite so cut and dried.

Mike was not, *could* not be, a cold-blooded killer.

He was kind. He was considerate.

He was also fit and strong. Tessa had seen him training the kids in the early autumn months. He had worn a vest and the muscles of his arms had been sharply defined.

Yes, he was strong; strong enough to hold a teenage girl underwater even if she struggled with all her might.

The TV droned quietly in the background, the sound so low that Tessa was able to hear the rumble of a vehicle engine outside, and the slushy sound of tyres coursing along the street.

For a moment she was frozen into place, thinking it was Mike but knowing that was crazy.

Quickly, she switched the lamps off and went to the window, inching back the curtain until she had a clear view of the lane.

A Land Rover had stopped on Church Road. Tessa recognised it immediately and stepped back, letting go of the curtain.

Now she remembered what had been nagging her about the conversation she'd had with Mike yesterday.

"Have you had any more dreams?"

"Uh-huh."

"No more details, nothing that would help?"

"I wish there was, Mike, I really do. The worst thing is, I feel like I'm so close to seeing whoever it was that held her down."

"And what would you do if you do get to see him?"

"I've been asking myself the same question. And the honest answer is, I don't know."

Now she knew. All the doubts in her mind had evaporated the moment she had seen the Land Rover parked outside.

Tessa had told him everything about the dream.

Shadows flickered in and out of existence. Tessa switched the TV off; she did not need its light to find the telephone.

What had gone through his mind when she had told him that she knew how Claire had died?

She reached out for the receiver and picked it up.

Had she sealed her own fate then? Had he encouraged her to keep talking just to find out how much she knew?

She pressed the receiver to her ear.

Or had he only decided he could not take any chances when Tessa had said she was so close to seeing the face of the killer? *His* face, though of course she had not known that then.

There was no dialling tone. The line was dead.

Somehow she had known that it would be.

Sure, the storm could have screwed everything up. At that moment Tessa could not be certain of anything.

With no signal for her mobile she had no way of raising the alarm.

From outside she could hear the crunch of footsteps in the snow, faint but drawing steadily closer.

Now she *was* certain. Mike was taking no chances.

All she could think of was that she had to get out. If she stayed here and Mike forced his way in, she'd be trapped.

Tessa hurriedly returned to the kitchen. She had left her walking boots by the back door overnight, letting melted snow dry into the mat. Now she tugged them on, struggling to knot the laces with trembling fingers. Her big coat was in the hall and it would have to stay there; she did not want him to see her through the glass. Her fleece was draped on the back of one of the kitchen chairs. She pulled it on and zipped it up. Then she took the key off its hook by the door and carefully inserted it into the lock.

Tessa winced as she turned the key; the sound seemed so loud that surely Mike must have heard it.

Of course he wouldn't. Even if he was halfway up the path the noise of his footsteps would have drowned out all else.

Tessa, heart racing, mouth powdery dry, pulled down the handle and eased the door open.

Without hesitation she stepped outside, wincing as her feet cracked the frozen surface of the snow. She pulled the door to but did not shut it tightly; her luck had held out so far but she did not want to risk making a sound.

As the door was towards the middle of the building she could not see the front of the house and Mike could not see her. Without waiting to find out how close he was she immediately set off along the path leading to the far end of the garden. Its boundary was marked by a chest-high wire fence. Beyond that was a narrow strip of snow-covered field leading to the trees.

A sudden loud rapping filled the air.

Tessa pictured Mike knocking impatiently at the front door, a well-rehearsed friendly look on his face, murder on his mind.

She was halfway along the garden now. It was unlikely he could hear her, especially with the noise he was making, so she increased her pace. There was always the danger she might slip and fall, but to her that was the lesser of two evils.

Moments later she reached the fence and clambered over it.

The nearest house was maybe a hundred yards away; she could be there in minutes, knocking on the door for help.

The only problem was that, as she headed towards it, so Mike would be able to see her. He would be able to intercept her before she reached it.

No, she thought. She needed to get past the tree line. With the forest to provide cover she could move quickly and unseen. It was then a question of travelling parallel to Church Road until she felt she was far enough away, and then she could drop down to the houses. Not even Mike would risk trying to stop her.

"Tessa!"

Until then she had felt almost unnaturally calm, like she was merely playing out a part in a play. But with the sound of his voice, carrying far and loud on the still morning air, came the realisation that this was no made-up drama and her life really was in danger.

She ran as quickly as she could across the open stretch of ground. It wasn't easy; the snow here was soft and deep and each step required such an effort that she soon began to tire.

"Tessa!"

The shout gave her new strength. Half of Bethesda must have heard him; he obviously didn't care.

And then the world dimmed as Tessa left daylight behind and plunged into the shadows of the forest.

She paused for a moment while she caught her breath. Each gasping exhalation conjured its own misty ghost. Her sudden burst of exertion had left Tessa hot and sweaty. Now the touch of air against her skin was a sharp reminder of just how cold it was. Her fingers began to tingle and she pushed her hands into her fleece pockets.

Tessa began to shiver. No matter how hard she tried, she could not make the trembling stop. The cold was intense and the only way to get warm was by moving.

She made herself start walking, thankful at least that the densely planted conifers had kept the ground relatively clear of snow. The going was much faster than it had been and it was not long before Tessa felt the worst of the shivers subside.

Caution had made her head deeper into the forest to begin with; there was a good chance Mike would spot her if she kept too close to the edge. There was no path for her to follow but the ground was flat and her boots found decent purchase even over the rougher stretches. When she felt she had gone deep enough, she changed direction, angling across the trees, fairly confident that she was more or less following the line of Church Road.

She would give it ten minutes, just to be safe, and then she would change direction again, dropping back down to Bethesda.

The crack of a branch snapping brought her sharply to a halt.

Tessa turned slowly round, peering into the half-light.

She could see nothing.

But she knew she hadn't imagined the sound.

Having failed to get an answer at the front door, there was a good chance Mike would have gone round to try the back.

Which, Tessa recalled with a sinking sensation, she had not pulled tightly shut in her haste to fly quietly away.

If he had hurried, Mike could have caught up with her by now. He would have had no problem knowing where she had gone, not with such an obvious trail of footprints to follow.

Panic gripped her. She could no longer think straight, had absolutely no idea what to do next.

And so she ran.

The forest floor was thickly carpeted with dead needles which absorbed most of the sound of her passage but even if every step had been as loud as a shotgun blast she would have kept on running anyway. She did not dare slow, did not dare look round. In her mind's eye Mike was right behind her, his superior fitness meaning he could comfortably follow until she had raced herself into the ground, ready for him to finish off.

Trees passed her in a blur. Her lungs hurt and her leg muscles began to burn. Despite her fear she knew she could not keep going much longer. Maybe it would be better to stop before she was too exhausted to even try to defend herself. Better yet, to find a branch, a rock, anything she could use as a weapon.

Then she burst out of the forest, into daylight.

The lake stretched out before her, grey and still.

Tessa managed to stop before she ran into the water.

This can't be happening, she told herself.

In her panic she had run the wrong way. Instead of racing towards Bethesda, as she had intended, she had been moving away from it. There was no hope of reaching safety now.

From behind she heard something move through the trees.

The sound was fairly distant. Tessa, poised to run, almost slumped with relief. It meant Mike had not caught up yet.

Now she at least had a chance of getting through this, Tessa found she could think clearly again. She looked along the path in both directions, determined to get her bearings before she moved off; she would not risk going the wrong way again.

The main track to Bethesda was to her right. Much closer, to her left, was the path that would take her to Hebron.

More importantly, it would take her *away* from Mike.

Satisfied she had made the right call, she began a slow jog towards the track. No breathless race this time. If she was careful and her luck held, she could be in Hebron in less than half an hour.

The path swung away from the lake, close to the forest edge.

As she passed the trees, so close that she could have reached out and touched them, a dark figure lunged out of the shadows. Before Tessa had time to cry out the figure barrelled straight into her, sending her sprawling.

Immediately she rolled and went to push herself to her feet, only to be struck a heavy blow against the back of her head which sent her face down into the hard ground. Pain exploded inside her mouth and she instantly tasted blood. Again she tried to regain her feet only to be hit down once more, this time the punch striking her temple with such force that her vision blurred. Another blow, to the stomach, left her unable to move, speak or try to fight her attacker off when she felt herself gripped by the shoulders and dragged to the water's edge. The world spun as she was hurled over, her face now to the sky. And then icy water closed over her head. The shock of it brought her fully round and she instinctively threw her arms upwards, trying to push him away but it was hopeless. She felt his hands on her shoulders, forcing her down. Terror gave her new strength and she began to violently thrash around. Still, though, she could not break free. Freezing water filled her nostrils. She coughed and began to choke. Now the water poured down her open mouth, driving out the last of the air in her lungs. Tessa began to weaken. *I'm dying*, she thought.

Above her the grey light seemed to grow brighter. It framed the dark shadow of her killer.

The dream was never about Claire.

It seemed so obvious now when it no longer mattered. A sense of peace stole through her, pushing the terror away. The cold faded, replaced by soothing warmth. Darkness encroached on her vision. She was dimly aware of the pressure on her shoulders lifting. And then it was as if her soul left her body behind and drifted to the surface. The water parted and she saw Mike was staring down at her, eyes wide, face contorted. He was shouting at her but the words were distorted, as if Tessa were still underwater.

She felt his hands on her chest, pushing.

And then there was a sudden rush through her guts and she jack-knifed, spewing water, coughing so harshly that it felt like her lungs were being ripped to shreds as she desperately swallowed air. It was cold but sweet and it cleared some of the fog from her head. The world had seemed so far away but now it zoomed into focus and she could feel Mike's arms around her, lifting her clear of the water. Tessa could do nothing for herself; she was like a puppet whose strings had been cut. She tried to speak but she had been struck dumb. Her body felt numb, either from shock or the iciness of the water. Shivers wracked her and she welcomed them; they meant she was still alive even if she did not quite feel it yet.

Her head, cradled in Mike's arms, lolled to one side as he lowered her gently to the ground. She could see a man sprawled out on the path a couple of yards away from her. His hair was grey and matted with dark blood which stained the snow around his head. A dark-smeared rock was on the ground next to him.

Tessa heard a rustling sound, and then the worst of the cold was gone. Through the mist in her head she sensed that Mike must have taken his coat off and wrapped it around her.

"Come on Tessa," she heard him say quietly, as if from a great distance away. "Let's get you out of here."

And then she was being lifted into the air. She could feel Mike's warm breath against her neck. Again she tried to speak only for her voice to fail her once more.

The world jogged around her as Mike carried her away from the lake. Suddenly she felt tremendously weary and she closed her eyes, meaning to rest them for just a moment or two.

It was the last thing she remembered.

His name was William Howard. He would be fifty years old next year and was divorced with two daughters that he saw regularly.

He was a travelling sales rep with an agricultural equipment manufacturing company, responsible for Wales and the West.

Police forensic evidence proved he had murdered a young woman in Bristol; a single mother who had gone for a walk in a local wood while her daughter was at school.

Her body was found the next day. She had been beaten and strangled to death before being raped.

Howard was also believed responsible for at least two other, similar killings; one in Devon and the other in Somerset. The DNA test results were awaited.

Detectives had reopened other unsolved cases from Wales and the West Country; and the North of England, where Howard had previously worked.

They would have plenty of questions to ask him, if and when he ever regained consciousness.

The blow that Mike had struck him with the rock had caused a fractured skull which in turn had led to swelling of the brain.

He was now in a coma.

Only time would tell if he would ever come out of it and, if so, whether there would be any serious permanent damage.

Tessa had learned all this lying in her own hospital bed.

Although her physical injuries had been comparatively superficial – cuts and bruises, a laceration in her scalp that required eight stitches – she had suffered hypothermia that led to a particularly virulent chest infection.

That, coupled with the media attention that the police wanted to deflect, had kept her in Brecon General.

It was now a week after the assault and the doctors had assured her she could go home within days, if she wanted.

She was not sure if she did. Her body was on the mend but the mental scars felt as if they were a long way from healing.

Mike had been to see her every day. On his first visit Tessa had cried and he had held her until she stopped.

They did not talk about what had happened, not until the third day. By then Mike had plenty to tell her.

Claire Marshall was home, alive and well. She had run off with an office manager named Robert Connolly, a Scotsman known to his wife and friends in Hebron as Robbie. As far as they knew, he had been sent on a course. In reality he had forced the teenager to go with him to a hotel in London. Claire had not wanted to go but was scared of what might happen if she refused.

Shortly after arriving she had burst into tears and insisted on calling her mother, to let her know she was safe. Connolly had used the threat of violence yet again to persuade her not to. Now she was back, having sneaked out of their hotel room early one morning with his stolen wallet while he slept, taking a taxi to Paddington and the next train home.

Connolly's wife had since moved out. The police had charged him with abduction and rape. Tessa was glad. The bastard deserved everything he got.

If there was any good to have come out of all this, it was the fact that Claire was okay, even if it would take a little while for mother and daughter to be fully reconciled.

The question was how long would it take Tessa to become fully reconciled with the fact that she screwed up so spectacularly?

She had made so many false assumptions along the way, the biggest perhaps being that she had dreamt of Claire's death.

Once the idea occurred to her there was never any room in her mind for doubt. She had never stopped to consider that perhaps she was not dreaming of Claire's fate but her own.

The dreams had been open to interpretation, as her dreams always were, and she had interpreted them wrongly.

Once the shock of the assault wore off, once Tessa had started coming to terms with the fact that she had survived an attack by a suspected serial killer, she began to piece together what she now believed to be the true meaning of her dreams.

The first part of it initially made no sense at all.

The burning sensation, the smell of smoke; what else was that supposed to indicate, if not a fire?

As the long hours passed and with nothing save her few permitted visitors to distract her, she began to play back the days, like a movie rewinding in her head.

And slowly the memories returned; the pieces of the jigsaw started falling into place.

Sitting at home last Monday morning, just hours before she would discover that Claire had gone missing, Tessa had been half asleep and half watching the TV; she remembered the newsreader saying something about a murder, about the possibility of Britain's first serial killer since the Yorkshire Ripper being on the loose.

That was when she had tipped scalding tea over her hand.

And entering the Fox and Hounds for her meeting with Mike, the air had been so thick with smoke that her eyes had stung.

A man had looked up as she walked in, a grey-haired man sitting alone, reading a newspaper. It had been William Howard. Tessa had since seen his picture.

Had he marked her down as his next victim, following her to Bethesda without her knowing?

Or had he by been in the woods by chance the day she had fled the house, taking up the opportunity that fate had so unexpectedly offered? Somehow Tessa doubted that; it was too much of a coincidence. Unless he came out of the coma and confessed, she would never know.

She'd overheard the loud men talk about Robert Connolly that same night, too, though of course she could not have known the significance of their conversation. None of his mates would have guessed that the story good old Robbie had put out was a lie.

She had dreamt of burning pain and of smoke.

She had assumed the dream was warning her of fire.

That, she thought, showed how wrong you could be.

She had been wrong about other things, such as assuming there was something suspicious about Greg Roberts being in Hebron. It transpired that he was, in fact, visiting his elderly mother who had suffered a stroke and was recovering at a convalescent home just outside the village. Greg, far from being sinister, now struck Tessa as a lonely, sad individual whose outwardly forceful personality was an over-compensation for his inner failings.

How glad she was that she had never called the police to give his name. It was bad enough knowing she had discussed her suspicions with Mike. She had made him swear not to say a word.

And as for Mike ... she could never tell him the truth about what had happened that fateful morning.

He had heard on the news that Claire had returned home. Phoning Tessa to make sure she knew too, he had discovered the line was dead and worried something might be wrong.

He had driven across cleared and snowbound roads alike to get to Bethesda. When he'd failed to get a response at the front door he had, as Tessa had thought he might – for all the wrong reasons – gone around and found the back door open.

That was when he had seen her footsteps.

He had followed, puzzled as to why she would be out in such conditions, leaving her home insecure. He had shouted her name once or twice and, not knowing where else to go, had decided he might just as well head for the lake.

It was just as well for her that he did.

Tessa had dodged the issue, telling Mike and the police that, feeling cooped up all alone in the cottage, she had decided to go for a walk. The open back door she had put down to forgetfulness.

They had no reason to doubt her; she was the victim after all.

It was late. Visiting time was nearly three hours ago. Mike had been there, as usual, even though Tessa had tried to tell him she would not mind in the least if he wanted to give it a miss one night; he had a long way to travel and the weather was foul. Though the snow had gone the rain that followed was heavy and persistent. But there was no persuading Mike. He said he would be there every night they kept her in. He had even offered to stay at the cottage with her when she returned home, until she felt she was up to being there alone. Tessa had promised to think about it.

And she would.

Secretly she was glad he insisted on being there every night. At first she thought that her gratitude was because she owed him a debt she could never repay. But then she realised that it was really because she genuinely liked him, and was in no doubt at all of his feelings towards her. Maybe it would lead to something beyond friendship; Tessa hoped it would, though she forbid herself from trying to imagine how it all might work out.

From now on she would never *ever* try to second-guess fate.

She had not dreamed since being brought into hospital.

If she did, Tessa told herself, she would put the dream to the back of her mind and wait for whatever would be.

She yawned, feeling desperately tired even though she had napped several times throughout the day. She reached out to switch off the bedside lamp before settling down with her eyes closed. Rain drummed steadily on the window behind her head and the wind howled like a beast in pain. Inside the room, though, it was so warm that Tessa could only tolerate a sheet over her, and she had pushed the lightweight quilt to the bottom of the bed.

From beyond the closed door she could hear occasional footsteps, low voices and the squeak of trolley wheels.

She welcomed them. They reminded her that there were people within calling distance, which in turn made her feel safe.

And, feeling safe, she slept.

STEVE LOCKLEY and PAUL LEWIS

Steve Lockley and Paul Lewis had enjoyed individual success as writers before teaming up in 1993 for the first of three volumes of the Cold Cuts horror anthology series.

They have gone on to collaborate on a series of stories including *The Winter Hunt*, which appeared in the *F20* anthology and was runner-up in the 2000 British Fantasy Awards; *Gabriel Restrained*, which appeared in *Darkness Rising: Hideous Dreams* and subsequently *Horrorfind* and *Best of Horrorfind;* and *Telling The Tale*, which appeared in *Urban Gothic: Lacuna and Other Trips*, and again was short listed for a British Fantasy Award.

Their first novel was the critically-acclaimed *The Ragchild* in 1999, short listed for a British Fantasy Award. The following year they created and edited the collaborative novella *In That Quiet Earth*.

Late 2002 saw the publication in the USA of *The Quarry*, a horror novel for young adults, while this year Lockley and Lewis saw their horror novella *King of All the Dead* published, with *The Ice Maiden* wrapping up a very successful and productive 12 months.

They are now working on several solo and collaborative projects.

Also Available from
www.pendragonpress.co.uk
or your local bookshop

Nasty Snips edited by Christopher C Teague
ISBN 0 9536833 0 3

Shenanigans by Noel K Hannan
ISBN 0 9538598 0 0

Tourniquet Heart edited by Christopher C Teague
ISBN 1 8948151 0 6
(*published by Prime Books*)

Other Books by Steve Lockley & Paul Lewis

As writers
The Ragchild
The Quarry
The King of all The Dead

As editors
Cold Cuts I, II, III
In that Quiet Earth
(also co-writers)